W9-BUB-784

BRANCH

MAXIMILIAN DOES IT AGAIN

MAXIMILIAN DOES IT AGAIN

. . . .

JOSEPH ROSENBLOOM

LODESTAR BOOKS

E. P. DUTTON ◆ NEW YORK

LIBRARY OF CONGRESS CATALOGING IN PUBLICATION DATA
Rosenbloom, Joseph
    Maximilian does it again.
    "Lodestar books."
    Summary: A collection of fourteen "case histories"
which Maximilian, the amazing twelve-year-old Manhattan
detective, was instrumental in solving.
[1. Mystery and detective stories] I. Title.
PZ7.R719176Mat 1983 [Fic] 82-18204
ISBN 0-525-67142-0

Published in the United States by E. P. Dutton, Inc.,
2 Park Avenue, New York, N.Y. 10016
Published simultaneously in Canada by Clarke,
Irwin & Company Limited, Toronto and Vancouver
Editor: Virginia Buckley   Designer: Trish Parcell
Printed in the U.S.A.   First Edition
10 9 8 7 6 5 4 3 2 1

• • • • • • • •

To Brian Marc Backerman

. . . .

CONTENTS

1
. . . .

THE CASE OF

The Dangerous Sidewalk

If you took a poll around Junior High School 28 in Manhattan and asked students how they rated various boys' names, the name Maximilian would rank as one of the worst. There actually was a boy named Maximilian in the school. His full name was Maximilian Augustus Adams.

How Maximilian hated his name! People were constantly making fun of it. Why couldn't he have been called Sam or Tom or Joe? It would have saved him tons of grief.

If the name Maximilian was unpopular, the boy himself was neither popular nor unpopular. In fact, the majority of students in Junior High School 28 hardly knew he existed.

Maximilian was polite enough, but he made no special

effort to be friendly. He seldom spoke unless first spoken to. Maximilian belonged to no clubs, was not interested in sports, had no hobbies. In short, the opinion around Junior High School 28 was that Maximilian was a dull fellow with a zero personality.

How wrong could you get! Maximilian was no ordinary twelve-year-old seventh-grade boy. If his fellow students were under the impression that he was an uninteresting fellow, it was because he preferred it that way. Maximilian had an unusual private life. He wanted very much to protect that private life against snoopers.

Maximilian's secret? Maximilian worked with members of the New York City Police Department in solving real crimes. Like Superman, who masqueraded as the harmless Clark Kent, Maximilian tried to blend into the woodwork. If anyone at Junior High School 28 so much as suspected that he worked with members of the New York City Police Department, it would only lead to problems. Better they should not know.

This extraordinary state of affairs came about quite by accident. Two years before, Maximilian built himself a shoeshine box. He worked around the neighborhood shining shoes until, one day, he discovered he could do a brisk business in front of the Mid-Manhattan Precinct House. A new precinct captain had taken over. The new captain turned out to be a stickler for neatness. He insisted that each police officer have shined shoes before going on duty. Every day, Maximilian therefore headed straight for the Mid-Manhattan Precinct House with his shoeshine box after school.

It was not long before the police officers at the precinct house became aware of Maximilian's unusual talents. His ability to grasp things was truly remarkable. His memory was unfailing and total. Maximilian was also a stupendous reader. He would devour books from the library by the armful.

While Maximilian enjoyed the friendship of most of the police officers, he felt especially close to Detective Walker. Detective Walker suspected that Maximilian had the brains and the talent to do police work. Detective Walker set out to teach Maximilian everything he knew. As a veteran of over twenty-three years of service as a police officer with the New York City Police Department, he knew plenty.

Maximilian took to police work like a duck takes to water. It was not long before Maximilian was a first-rate detective in his own right.

One February afternoon, Detective Walker and Maximilian were hurrying to the post office to get there before it closed. On their way, they saw a small crowd in front of the Cinderella Beauty Salon. The Cinderella Beauty Salon was favored by celebrities from the world of theater and fashion and by pampered society ladies.

Mr. John, owner of the beauty salon, was in great demand. You could get an appointment with one of his many assistants easily enough, but an appointment with Mr. John was another matter. For Mr. John to do your hair, you had to make an appointment months in advance.

Detective Walker and Maximilian stopped to investigate the reason for the crowd.

3

There on the ground lay a woman clutching her right leg. The woman wore a ridiculous wig that looked like a glob of cotton candy. The wig was several sizes too large and kept slipping over her eyes. On the sidewalk near the woman lay the contents of three shopping bags.

Detective Walker identified himself as a police officer. He tried to find out what had happened. It was hard to get information out of the woman because she seemed to be in great pain. Besides, every time she tried to talk, her wig slipped off her head and covered her eyes. She had to stop to put the wig right. She finally pointed to a patch of ice and told Detective Walker that she had slipped on it.

Detective Walker glanced at her injured leg. Her stocking was torn, but there seemed to be no bleeding. All he could see was an ugly black-and-blue mark on her shin. Detective Walker asked the woman if she wanted an ambulance. The woman adjusted her wig and said she did not think she needed one. She then tried to stand up with Detective Walker's assistance, but her leg buckled and she sank back to the ground, howling with pain.

Mr. John came outside to see why a crowd had gathered in front of his beauty salon. He shrieked with horror at the sight of the woman lying on the ground.

"Oh, dear! Oh, dear me!" he cried, wringing his hands. "What happened?"

Detective Walker explained that the woman had taken a nasty fall on the patch of ice in front of his beauty salon.

Mr. John felt dizzy as the blood drained from his face. "I think I'm going to get sick," he announced. "I'm going to faint!" He clutched his heart.

Mr. John had every reason to be upset. Just the other day an inspector from the Department of Sanitation had handed him a ticket for having an icy sidewalk. The inspector warned him that the ice should be cleared off the sidewalk before someone got hurt. Mr. John had intended to have his handyman remove the dangerous patch of ice, but, as luck would have it, the handyman came down with the flu and went home early. Mr. John became so busy in the Cinderella Beauty Salon with customers, he honestly forgot about the patch of ice. However, that wouldn't help him much if the woman decided to sue him. Why, if she wanted to, Mr. John realized to his horror, she could take him for every cent he was worth.

The howls of pain grew louder and more frequent. Mr. John winced everytime the woman screamed. "Please," he pleaded with her. "Please, madam, do try to keep your voice lower. You are attracting attention. What will people think?"

The woman did not seem to care what people thought. She kept on screaming.

Mr. John hated unpleasantness of any sort. And this, he decided, was definitely unpleasant. If he closed his eyes and wished hard enough, perhaps she would disappear. He closed his eyes and wished as hard as he had ever wished for anything in his entire life. When he opened his eyes, however, there she still was—still

5

flat on the ground—and still yelling at the top of her lungs.

A distinguished-looking gentleman carrying a small black bag edged his way through the crowd. Detective Walker asked the man if he was a doctor. "Yes, I am," he said. "My name is Dr. Melvin R. Harris. I have an office around the corner."

The doctor bent over to examine the injured woman. He touched her leg ever so gently. She let out an ear-piercing howl. Poor Mr. John jumped three feet straight up in the air. The doctor suggested they move the woman out of the cold and into the store where he could examine her more thoroughly. Dr. Harris, Detective Walker, Mr. John, and Maximilian helped to carry the woman into the Cinderella Beauty Salon.

After the woman was made comfortable, Detective Walker continued to question her.

"What is your name, please?" he asked.

"Babs Smith," she answered weakly.

"Where do you live, Babs?"

"Here and there. No place in particular."

Detective Walker guessed that the woman was a bag lady. A bag lady is one of those homeless women who wander around the streets of big cities. They carry all their worldly possessions in their shopping bags.

Detective Walker apologized. He said he had to get to the post office before it closed. The woman pleaded with him not to go. Detective Walker patted her hand. He told her not to worry. "The doctor will take good care of you. Won't you, doctor?" Dr. Harris smiled reassuringly. Detective Walker promised the woman he would stop by later to check on how she was doing.

Detective Walker thought his errand at the post office would take only a few minutes. It took well over a half hour. By the time Detective Walker and Maximilian returned to the Cinderella Beauty Salon, the doctor and the injured woman had gone.

"When did the woman leave?" Detective Walker asked. Mr. John said that she had just left.

"Any problems?"

"None. I took care of the whole business in a most satisfactory manner." Mr. John beamed, immensely pleased with himself.

"Oh?" Detective Walker raised an eyebrow.

"Dr. Harris said it was a compound fracture. He said her right leg had been broken in two places. Would you believe that nasty woman actually threatened to sue me? She said the accident was my fault. Why didn't I keep the sidewalk in front of my beauty salon free of ice so that people could walk the street in safety? Luckily, I did some pretty fast talking and got her to change her mind about suing me."

"How did you manage that?"

Mr. John looked first this way, then that way. "Can you keep a secret?" he asked.

"Maybe," Detective Walker said.

"I made a deal. I gave her $2,500 to settle the matter quietly between ourselves. She took the money and promised to drop the matter. Clever of me, wasn't it?"

Mr. John's story set the wheels of Maximilian's mind

turning. He concentrated so hard, his brows creased and the lids of his eyes narrowed until they were mere slits.

It was not very long before the expression on his face relaxed. He had found the missing clue.

Maximilian reached into the right back pocket of his pants and took out a small notebook. Maximilian called this notebook, which he always carried, a memo book. All police officers carry a memo book when they are on duty. Maximilian had his own memo book like a regular police officer.

After writing in his memo book, Maximilian handed it to Detective Walker. Detective Walker read the entry and smiled. "Maximilian," he said, "you've done it again! Another piece of incredible detective work."

Maximilian blushed a deep red.

Turning to Mr. John, Detective Walker said, "Mr. John, I have some unpleasant news for you. That fall in front of your beauty salon was a fake. The woman was not hurt. It was all staged. Nor was the doctor a real doctor. I'm afraid you've been taken."

Mr. John was not convinced. "But what about her bloodcurdling screams?"

"Anyone can scream loud."

"But how about that big black-and-blue mark on her shin?"

"Stage makeup."

Mr. John still had his doubts. "You can't prove it, can you?"

Detective Walker did not bother to reply. Instead, he showed Maximilian's memo book to Mr. John.

Mr. John read the memo book and was stunned. He hung his head in shame. "And I thought I was being so clever." He sighed.

Detective Walker, who always had a riddle to tell, tried to cheer Mr. John up. "That reminds me of a riddle," he said. "Why did the lady with straight hair jump in the ocean?"

"I don't know," Mr. John said. "Why?"

"Because she wanted a wave in her hair."

How did Maximilian know the fall was faked?
(See page 118.)

2
· · · · · · · ·
THE CASE OF
The Thirteenth
Richest Man

Mr. John of the Cinderella Beauty Salon was not the only victim of the bag lady and her phony doctor companion. A number of other businesses had been similarly fleeced over the past several days.

The police were on the lookout for the pair. One officer jokingly referred to the woman as Babs the Bag Lady. The name stuck.

Babs the Bag Lady and the fake doctor sensed that the police were on their trail. No matter. The world was full of suckers. They simply moved their operations uptown to the East Side where the rich lived.

Although the streets were no longer icy, most sidewalks in New York City had at least one hole or crack on which a nasty fall could be blamed. Babs the Bag

Lady found a satisfactory crack in front of a mansion on 65 Street. She looked up and down the block to make sure no one was around, spilled the contents of her three shopping bags on the ground, sat down on the sidewalk, adjusted her wig, cleared her throat, and gave forth with ear-splitting howls.

It was not long before a crowd gathered around her. Everyone clucked sympathetically and was eager to be of help. Babs the Bag Lady was in excellent form that day. Her screams would have done an opera credit.

After one particularly bloodcurdling scream, a curtain in the elegant mansion parted ever so slightly. One eye peered out. The eye belonged to Lucas, companion and secretary to Mr. H. Henry Hunt. Mr. Hunt was a very rich old man. He was reputed to be the thirteenth richest man in the world.

The curtain closed again. Lucas hoped that if the woman were ignored she would go away. Little did he know Babs the Bag Lady. She had an incredible pair of lungs. She could keep screaming until your eardrums begged for mercy.

Dr. Melvin R. Harris, as usual, made his appearance at just the right moment. Yes, her leg was broken. Yes, it was a compound fracture. Her leg was broken in two places. He insisted the fallen woman be brought inside the elegant mansion. He rang the bell. No answer. He rang again. Still no answer. The doctor took to pounding on the door with his fists. Finally, Lucas opened the door a crack.

"What do you want?" he snapped. "If you're selling anything, we don't want any!" Lucas tried to slam the door shut, but the doctor was too quick for him. He deftly jammed his foot in the door.

The doctor glared at Lucas. "I have an injured woman out there. She tripped over a crack in your sidewalk. I am a medical doctor, and I warn you, her condition is critical. I will hold you personally responsible if there are complications. I demand that you open the door at once!"

Lucas refused. "I can't allow such riffraff into this house." He crinkled his nose in distaste. "Why, she is nothing but a common bag lady!"

The crowd did not care for Lucas's attitude. "She is a human being!" one person shouted. "I hope they throw you in jail!" another yelled, shaking his fist. "You have no heart!" a third jeered. Then the entire crowd took to booing and hissing Lucas.

Babs the Bag Lady, encouraged by the support of the bystanders, found her voice and began to howl again. With each scream, the crowd became more threatening. There was no telling what a crowd in such an ugly mood might do. Lucas thought it advisable to allow the woman inside, no matter how distasteful he found her. He would get rid of the woman as soon as the crowd disappeared.

Once inside the house, Dr. Melvin R. Harris resumed his examination. He confirmed the woman had a compound fracture caused by a fall over a crack in the sidewalk.

Lucas went to fetch Mr. Hunt, his employer, who was

in another part of the house. H. Henry Hunt stormed into the room, took one look at the woman and the doctor, and decided he did not like either.

"Who let these people into my house?" He scowled.

Lucas gulped. "I did, sir."

H. Henry Hunt fixed an icy stare on Lucas.

"I had to!" Lucas cringed. "The woman fell on our sidewalk. She broke her leg."

"In two places," added the doctor.

"Who cares? Probably serves her right, anyhow. The old hag!"

Babs the Bag Lady reacted violently. "Who are you calling an old hag, you miserable old goat, you! I'll sue you for everything you've got!"

H. Henry Hunt snapped his fingers in her face. "Go ahead and sue. See if I care."

Something like this had never happened before. In Babs the Bag Lady's long career of fleecing people, always the victim had been eager to pay to get rid of her. How was she to know that old H. Henry Hunt was as tightfisted as they come? People said he still had the first dollar he had ever made.

Babs the Bag Lady had met her match. Neither would budge an inch.

"I'm warning you!" Babs the Bag Lady shook her finger.

"Who asked you to walk on my sidewalk?" H. Henry Hunt snorted.

"I'll sue you!"

H. Henry Hunt turned to Lucas. "It's all your fault,

Lucas! I'm going upstairs to take a bath now. By the time I come downstairs again, I expect the matter to have been settled and those awful people long since out of my house. Is that understood, Lucas?"

"Yes, sir." Lucas gulped. "I'll do my best."

"I doubt that!" H. Henry Hunt sneered.

"Enjoy your warm bath and nap!" Dr. Melvin R. Harris called after Mr. Hunt.

"Warm bath!" H. Henry Hunt humphed. "Young man, heating water costs money. I will take a cold bath, thank you! A nap, that I can take. It doesn't cost anything."

Mr. Hunt creaked up the stairs, leaving Lucas alone to settle the messy problem.

Lucas and Babs the Bag Lady began to bargain. Lucas made an offer of $500. She laughed in his face. He upped the figure to $750. She still laughed in his face. For someone who had just sustained a compound fracture, Babs the Bag Lady displayed amazing stamina. They bargained on and on. They finally settled on $1,000.

Lucas opened a safe hidden behind a painting and took out $1,000 in cash. He looked miserable as he handed it to Babs the Bag Lady. Lucas dreaded what Mr. Hunt would say when he learned about the money.

"Don't be upset," Babs the Bag Lady told Lucas. "I'm letting you off easy. I'm really doing you a big favor."

Lucas wasn't so sure.

Babs the Bag Lady then placed her arm around the shoulders of the fake doctor. She made faces that would make a rock bleed as she slowly limped out of the house.

14

When H. Henry Hunt learned that Lucas had given the woman $1,000, he turned ugly. He screamed that Lucas was a crook, always had been. He swore to take the money out of Lucas's salary. He attacked Lucas again and again. People who were unfortunate enough to be around H. Henry Hunt when he was in this mood said they had seen sharks with kinder faces.

How could Lucas have tolerated such abuse? Why did he put up with H. Henry Hunt for twenty long, bleak, unhappy years? He did so only because Mr. Hunt, having no living relatives, had promised to leave his entire fortune to Lucas. The dream of possessing such vast wealth is what kept him going. Lucas told himself every day that his cruel situation could not go on forever. H. Henry Hunt was a sick man. How much longer could he live? And when the old man died, Lucas would inherit his many millions.

Then the one thing Lucas dreaded most in all the world happened. H. Henry Hunt was so angry at Lucas for having given the Bag Lady $1,000, he declared he was going to alter his will. All his millions would go to charity.

Lucas saw red. The rage that had been building up over the years could no longer be held in check. Something inside him snapped. A poker that had been in the fireplace suddenly found itself in his hand. It came down over old H. Henry Hunt's head with a powerful blow. H. Henry Hunt sank to the floor.

When Lucas regained his senses and realized what he had done, he frantically tried to cover up the evidence.

Only after he was satisfied that no trace of suspicion would lead back to him did he call the police.

Detective Walker responded to the call. He found H. Henry Hunt, formerly the thirteenth richest man in the world, dead on the floor. The murder weapon was next to the body. The room, which was the library, was in shambles. Books and papers were scattered about everywhere. Some were on top of the body. Detective Walker began to question Lucas.

"When did you last see Mr. Hunt alive?"

"Early this afternoon. Mr. Hunt had gone upstairs for a bath and a nap. I waited for him to fall asleep and then went out to do some shopping."

"How long were you gone from the house?"

"About an hour, I should say. When I got back, I heard a groan coming from the library. I went in to investigate. There I found Mr. Hunt on the floor."

"Was he still alive?"

"Yes. However, before he died, he managed to tell me what had happened. He told me he had been napping but was awakened by noises coming from the library. He said he went downstairs to investigate. In the library he found two burglars going through his desk and files. They were masked, but he could tell it was a man and a woman. He said the man attacked him with a poker. Then the intruders fled."

"Did Mr. Hunt have enemies?"

Lucas hesitated for a moment. He decided the truth would serve him best now. "Did he have enemies! That's a laugh. To know Mr. Hunt was to loathe him. Even I despised him. He was a miserable old miser."

"Has anything out of the ordinary happened in the neighborhood lately?"

Lucas was hoping for a question like this. Here was a chance to throw Detective Walker off.

"Come to think of it, something unusual did happen this morning. A woman fell in front of our house. We brought her inside. A doctor said she had a compound fracture. The woman said it was our fault. She said she tripped over a large crack in our sidewalk. She threatened to sue us. I gave her money to get rid of her."

"Did the woman happen to be carrying shopping bags filled with all kinds of junk?"

"Why yes!" Lucas was amazed. "How did you know?"

"And was the doctor named Dr. Melvin R. Harris?"

Lucas nodded in surprise.

"That, my friend, was Babs the Bag Lady and her phony doctor pal. They have been working the streets with fake falls. People would rather pay them off than go through the trouble of going to court. The pair make a handsome living staging their little shows."

"Oh, dear!" Lucas bit his lip. "Mr. Hunt warned me not to pay her anything. It just never occurred to me this could be a racket. They acted so convincingly."

"They've had lots of practice. How much did she get Mr. Hunt for?"

"She got $1,000."

"Only $1,000!" Detective Walker whistled. "That's cheap. She usually gets lots more."

"That may be. But Mr. Hunt was furious with me. He said I had given her too much. She didn't think so. She said $1,000 was not nearly enough to pay for her pain

17

and anguish. When Mr. Hunt refused to give her any more, she turned nasty. She said she would get even with him one day."

Lucas brightened as if a remarkable idea had suddenly occurred to him. "Say, you don't suppose the burglars could have been the bag lady and the fake doctor?"

"Life is full of surprises, Lucas. Anything is possible."

Detective Walker thanked Lucas for his cooperation and returned to the Mid-Manhattan Precinct House.

Maximilian was munching on a chocolate bar to restore his drooping energy after a long day in school, when Detective Walker arrived.

"Our friend Babs the Bag Lady and her pal, the fake doctor, have been at it again," Detective Walker remarked. "This time they fleeced old H. Henry Hunt out of $1,000. Unfortunately, someone also did away with him."

"Any leads?" Maximilian asked.

"Nothing solid." Detective Walker than gave Maximilian a rundown on the case. As Detective Walker spoke, Maximilian's expression changed. His brows creased and his eyes narrowed until they were almost shut. Maximilian was concentrating hard. However, his expression soon relaxed. He took out his memo book and wrote in it. He then showed Detective Walker what he had written.

Detective Walker smiled as he read. "Maximilian," he said, "I'm proud of you. That is first-class detective work!"

Maximilian hoped no one saw him blush.

Detective Walker proceeded to H. Henry Hunt's residence where Lucas was arrested and charged with murder.

Lucas quickly confessed when shown the evidence.

"That reminds me of a riddle," Detective Walker said. "What did the little chicken say to the miser?"

"I don't know," Lucas replied. "What?"

"Cheap! Cheap!"

Lucas thought the riddle was very appropriate.

How did Maximilian know Lucas was guilty?
(See page 119.)

3

· · · · · · · ·

THE CASE OF

The Graffiti
Phantom

Maximilian worked more and more outside the precinct house on cases with Detective Walker. This created a problem. Who would shine the officers' shoes while Maximilian was away? Maximilian needed an assistant. He selected Peter Wolfe.

Peter Wolfe was also twelve years old and in the same seventh-grade class at Junior High School 28. Although Peter and Maximilian were good friends, they argued a good deal. One of the main things they argued about was how to solve crimes. Maximilian thought that every criminal gave himself away when a fact in the case did not hold up. Identify the error in fact, and you were well on the way to solving the case. This is why Maximilian stuffed his head with all kinds of facts. You never knew when some obscure piece of information would be what you needed to solve a case.

Peter disagreed. According to Peter, it was logic, not facts, that was the true key to solving crimes. Every case involved an error in logic. Find the error in logic, and you solve the crime.

Peter was also an inventor. After trying to make a perpetual motion machine, without success, he turned to inventing a crime-solving computer. Feed information about a case into this special computer, press a button, and—presto!—you crack the case. Maximilian said it couldn't be done. Peter went on building his crime-solving computer anyhow.

Peter called his computer CLAM. CLAM was short for Crime Logic Analyzing Machine. The first version did not work at all; the second one caused an explosion; the third one set off a fire. Peter was too determined to allow such insignificant problems to stand in his way. He was now working on the fourth version.

Maximilian and Peter were walking to the precinct house one afternoon after school. Maximilian was munching on a chocolate bar as usual. They made an odd couple. Maximilian was of medium height and plump. Peter was a full head taller and as thin as a rail. Maximilian was a careful dresser. He wore a spotless shirt with a pink polka-dotted bow tie. His trousers were pressed and his shoes shined. He had a scrubbed appearance. Peter was a slob by comparison. Most of the time, he looked like an unmade bed. When he was inventing things, which pretty much was always, he couldn't be bothered with such things as clean clothes or neatness.

Maximilian had an embarrassing duty to perform. The precinct captain had complained about Peter's sloppiness. He was setting a bad example for the men, the precinct captain said. Since Peter was Maximilian's assistant, it was up to Maximilian to straighten Peter out.

Peter was feeling low after Maximilian lectured him. The very last person in the world Peter wanted to see just then turned up. It was his sister, Jessica. Jessica was ten years old and in the fifth grade at P.S. 42, nearby.

Ever since Peter began to work at the precinct house, Jessica had been pestering Maximilian. She also wanted to be Maximilian's assistant. Maximilian told her no. He said there were already two young people around the precinct house, Peter and himself. A third would be out of the question.

Jessica accused Maximilian of discriminating against her on the basis of age. Just because she was two years younger than Maximilian or Peter didn't mean she couldn't handle the work. Maximilian denied discriminating against her on the basis of age. She then accused him of practicing discrimination on the basis of sex. He didn't want her around because she was a girl. Maximilian denied that he was a sexist. Jessica kept after Maximilian. She wore him down. He finally agreed that if and when Peter left the precinct house, she could have his job.

Jessica was not satisfied. "But what about now?" She pouted.

Maximilian had an idea. "Suppose I gave you lessons in detective work in the meantime?"

Jessica grinned happily. "You've just made yourself a deal! When do we start?"

"Next week?"

"Next week!" she protested. "Look, if we're going to do it, let's do it! How about today?"

"Okay." Maximilian sighed. "We'll meet tonight after dinner and get started."

Peter did not think much of Jessica's future as a detective. "You're wasting your time trying to teach her anything," Peter said to Maximilian. "She's so stupid, she even flunked recess."

Jessica glared. "Close your mouth, Peter, before someone stuffs an apple in it."

"If it weren't for your stupidity, you'd have no personality at all," Peter snapped.

"Did you ever think of checking into a home for the chronically strange?" Jessica replied.

Maximilian silently slipped away as Jessica and Peter continued to hurl their insults at each other. He had read enough books on psychology to recognize that this feuding pair suffered from what the psychologists called sibling rivalry. Whatever Peter had, Jessica wanted; whatever Jessica had, Peter wanted. Maximilian could do nothing about it. Being caught in the middle made him feel uncomfortable.

The next morning Mr. Patterson, the principal of Junior High School 28, called a special assembly. He announced that someone, as yet unidentified, had scribbled graffiti on the school walls. Mr. Patterson knew that once graffiti began to appear, it would only lead to still more graffiti. He had been to schools where there was so much graffiti on the walls, you couldn't tell the original color of the walls anymore. He did not want the same thing to happen at his school. Mr. Patterson was using the assembly to warn whoever was doing it to stop, and to caution others who might have similar ideas not to start.

Every school has its bully. In Junior High School 28 it was Timothy McGee, otherwise known as Sluggo. He got his nickname because he would rather hit than talk. Sluggo's main problem was that his body was too big for his brain.

Sluggo hated Maximilian. Maximilian had once gotten Sluggo in trouble with Mr. Patterson. Sluggo had stolen a stamp album from a school locker and Maximilian had helped catch him. Sluggo vowed he would get even.

Sluggo scribbled a huge graffiti near Mr. Patterson's office. The graffiti read in black, hand-printed letters, MAXIMILIAN STINKS! Sluggo guessed it would only be a matter of time before Maximilian would hear about the graffiti and attempt to remove it. He was right. Someone told Maximilian about the graffiti. When Maximilian read what it said, he found a rag, wet it in the school fountain, and tried to rub the graffiti off.

Sluggo dashed to the principal's office and told Mr. Patterson to hurry if he wanted to catch the Graffiti Phantom in action. Mr. Patterson and Sluggo rushed to the spot. There they saw Maximilian doing something to the wall.

"What on earth are you doing, Maximilian?" Mr. Patterson demanded.

Maximilian spun around and got the surprise of his life seeing Mr. Patterson behind him.

"Why, uh, nothing!" Maximilian sputtered.

"I repeat. What are you doing, young man?"

"I, uh, am trying to remove this graffiti, sir."

"Listen, pal, you're the Graffiti Phantom," Sluggo declared knowingly. "So why don't you knock it off!"

"I am not!"

It was then that Sluggo noticed something and whispered in Mr. Patterson's ear.

"What is that sticking out of your pocket?" Mr. Patterson asked.

It turned out to be a black Magic Marker. Mr. Patterson demanded to know why Maximilian carried a black Magic Marker. Maximilian said he needed the Magic Marker to finish a poster in his art class. Mr. Patterson sadly asked Maximilian to come along to his office. It pained him greatly to think that of all the students in his school, Maximilian might be the Graffiti Phantom.

Behind the closed doors of Mr. Patterson's office, Maximilian was again asked to explain what he was doing at the wall. Maximilian stuck to his story. He was trying to wipe the graffiti off the wall, he insisted. As for the black Magic Marker, he needed it to finish a poster. Mr. Patterson could check with Maximilian's art teacher if he liked.

Maximilian was then told to wait outside while Sluggo was asked to come into the principal's office. Mr. Patterson told Sluggo that Maximilian had denied writing the graffiti.

"He's lying!" Sluggo protested loudly. "I *know* Maximilian is the Graffiti Phantom. Don't let him fool you."

"But what I don't understand is, why should he write MAXIMILIAN STINKS!" Mr. Patterson wondered. "It's been my experience that graffiti-scribbling is basically an ego trip. You say nice things about yourself. You might say bad things, but then only about someone else."

Sluggo scratched his head. He found it hard to think fast. "Maybe Maximilian wrote the graffiti to throw you off. That's it! He's a smart cookie. If Maximilian wrote something bad about himself, then maybe you wouldn't suspect he was the Graffiti Phantom."

"I doubt that. In fact, nothing you have said up until now leads me to believe that Maximilian is the person we are looking for."

"But Mr. Patterson!" Sluggo said in a voice betraying anxiety. He felt Maximilian was slipping off the hook. "I saw him do it with my own two eyes. Honest! I was there before Maximilian got to the wall. I saw everything from beginning to end."

"How long were you there before Maximilian?"

"At least five minutes."

"Which might have given you enough time to scribble the graffiti yourself."

"Why do I always get blamed for everything that goes wrong around this school!" Sluggo whined in a high-pitched voice. "It isn't fair!" He sensed that Mr. Patterson suspected him now. How quickly the tables had turned. Poor Sluggo's brain couldn't figure out where he had gone wrong.

Maximilian, who had been waiting in the hallway, was asked to return to the office.

"Well, gentlemen," Mr. Patterson said, "it appears both of you deny being the Graffiti Phantom. I believe that one of you is lying."

"It's not me!" Sluggo declared emphatically.

Maximilian did not reply. He was too busy concentrating. Sluggo was guilty, of course, but how could he prove it? He concentrated so hard, his brow creased and his eyes narrowed until he could hardly see through them. The answer finally came. He asked Mr. Patterson for a sheet of paper. Maximilian printed MAXIMILIAN STINKS! on it. He then demanded that Sluggo do the same. Within minutes, Mr. Patterson knew the identity of the Graffiti Phantom. There could be no doubt about it. It was Sluggo.

How did Maximilian prove Sluggo was guilty?
(See page 120.)

4

· · · · · · ·

THE CASE OF

The Cross-eyed Gaucho

Detective Walker and Maximilian turned the corner of 46 Street when they spotted a familiar figure. It was Benny the Onion. He was talking a mile a minute, arms flapping about wildly like a windmill. Benny was trying to get a man to buy the object Benny clutched in his right hand. The man listened, considered for a moment, and decided that he did not want to buy the object. He walked off leaving Benny to look for another customer. Benny found a new one within seconds. Benny launched into his sales pitch again with undiminished enthusiasm.

Benny the Onion got his nickname because he always had a sad story to tell. His tales of woe were so convincing, they made people cry as if they were peeling onions. People felt so sorry for him they often reached into their pockets and gave him money. This is how he managed to stay alive.

If Benny the Onion was good at telling sad stories, the one thing he was not good at was keeping whatever little money he managed to get his hands on. Every dollar Benny had went right into some hare-brained scheme or other. No matter how wild, no matter how impractical, no matter how dishonest the scheme—Benny the Onion would fall for it. Benny was always broke, as a result. If you asked him which American president was on a one-dollar bill, he really couldn't tell you. Benny never held on to one long enough to find out.

Benny was so busy trying to sell the object in his hand, he failed to see Detective Walker and Maximilian coming up from behind.

The sudden appearance of Detective Walker and Maximilian took Benny the Onion by surprise. He tried to hide the object he was selling behind his back. "Why Detective Walker and Maximilian!" He grinned nervously. "How nice to see you again. I hope you are both well."

"Okay, Benny," Detective Walker said, "cut the act. Where did you get it?"

"Get what?" Benny said, his eyes opening wide in innocence.

"The thing behind your back."

"Oh, you mean this!" Benny said as if he hadn't the faintest idea how the object could have gotten into his hand.

"Let's have it, Benny!" Detective Walker demanded.

Benny handed the object over. It was an old photograph set in a handsome silver frame. The picture was that of a South American cowboy, a gaucho. He wore a poncho over one shoulder, a jacket, and a bright shirt. In one hand he held a *bola*. The *bola* was used by the gauchos to capture animals and cattle. It consisted of two or more heavy balls attached to stout cords. The *bola* was thrown at an animal, and, by entwining about the legs, it brought the animal down. The man in the picture was not unpleasant looking, but he was extremely cross-eyed.

"Who is the man in the picture?" Detective Walker asked.

Benny the Onion gazed fondly at the photograph. "That, Detective Walker, is my beloved great-grandfather."

Benny wiped an invisible tear from his eye, sighed, and bravely continued.

"This handsome silver frame and the picture have been in my family for three generations. My great-grandfather's name was Hector Gonzales Balthazar Gomez. He was a gaucho in Argentina."

Detective Walker gave Benny one of his I-don't-believe-a-word-you're-saying stares.

"Would I lie to you?" Benny sounded offended.

Detective Walker was about to reply yes but checked himself. After all, Benny told such entertaining tales, perhaps it would be fun to let him go on. "I'm all ears," Detective Walker said.

"It was the winter of 1888," Benny began. "In that

year the American ambassador to Argentina was visiting the ranch on which my great-grandfather worked as a gaucho. The ambassador asked to be shown the herds of cattle scattered over the ranch. My great-grandfather volunteered to accompany the American ambassador.

"While they were in the most desolate part of the ranch, the sky suddenly darkened. A midwinter blizzard struck without warning. They were miles from any shelter. Curiously, on the very same day, March 12, 1888, a terrible blizzard also hit New York City." Benny turned to Maximilian, "Isn't that so?" Maximilian verified that a record snowfall had indeed fallen on New York City on March 12, 1888.

"Thank you," Benny the Onion said, pleased that Maximilian had confirmed his statement.

"Unlike my great-grandfather, who was accustomed to the rugged life on the Argentinian pampas, the American ambassador was a city man. The wind and snow affected him quickly. He began to shiver. My great-grandfather threw his poncho over the ambassador. It helped, but not for long. My great-grandfather then gave the ambassador his jacket and finally his vest. The ambassador still suffered greatly from the cold. The situation was turning more and more desperate. If help did not arrive soon, the ambassador was doomed.

"My great-grandfather took one last gamble. He wrote a note and pinned it to the saddle of his horse, Blanco. He then whispered into the horse's ear. 'Blanco,' he said, 'you must reach the ranch house and get help. If you do not get help, the American will freeze to death. Do you understand, Blanco?' The horse neighed as if he understood every word. Blanco set off through the howling blizzard for the ranch house."

"And did Blanco get through?" Detective Walker asked.

"Miraculously, yes. The American ambassador and my great-grandfather were rescued—but just in the nick of time. The ambassador was so grateful, he gave my great-grandfather money for passage to the United States. And that, my friends, is how my family came to be Americans."

Benny the Onion sighed. "I would sooner part with this beautiful picture than with my right hand. But what can I do? I need the money because I have to . . ."

Maximilian tried to muffle the giggle forming in his throat, but failed. The sound spilled through his fingers. Benny's voice trailed off as he heard the giggle. Benny was hurt and insulted. It was one thing for a grown-up to question one of his stories; it was quite another for a mere twelve-year-old boy to do so. "And what is so amusing about my story?" Benny demanded. "I don't hear anyone else laughing."

Maximilian apologized. "I'm sorry, Benny, if I've offended you. It's just that facts are facts."

"Are you suggesting my story about the photograph is untrue? Okay, you're supposed to be the great detective. Prove it!"

Benny crossed his arms and waited for Maximilian to answer his challenge.

Maximilian opened his memo book and wrote in it. He then showed what he had written to Benny.

"I didn't know that!" Benny the Onion said surprised. "You learn something new every day. You really are a great detective, Maximilian."

Maximilian blushed.

"This reminds me of a riddle," Detective Walker said. "Why was the photographer arrested?"

"I don't know," Benny said. "Why?"

"Because he shot people and then tried to blow them up."

Why was Benny the Onion's story false?
(See page 121.)

5

· · · · · · · ·

THE CASE OF
The Missing
Ten Commandments

Detective Walker's twenty-one-year-old daughter, Jean, worked as a cub reporter on the *New York Evening Star*. At first, she considered herself lucky to have landed a job on one of the city's largest newspapers fresh out of journalism school. Now, she wasn't so sure.

You would expect a small-town newspaper to print news about social events such as weddings and parties, but not one of the major newspapers in New York City. That's what Jean also thought before she went to work for the *New York Evening Star*. She was soon to learn that people in New York City were interested in much the same kinds of things as people in small towns. Her main job was to cover weddings, parties, engagements, and similar social functions. It did not matter that she thought these events were unimportant. Someone had to cover them for her newspaper. As the newest member of the staff, she was it.

Jean pleaded with her boss to give her more challenging assignments. Why couldn't she cover wars, revolutions, assassinations? Her boss said no. He told her to be patient. He promised Jean she would get more important assignments—eventually. In the meantime, he advised her to keep her eyes and ears open and learn as much as she could. Poor Jean. The days dragged on.

Jean's boss dropped a letter on her desk one day. "Check this out," he told her and walked off without another word.

Jean opened the envelope and removed a brief letter written in a beautiful script. The letter said the writer knew the whereabouts of the original Tablets of the Law on which the Ten Commandments were written. The writer asked someone on the newspaper to call on him for further information. The letter was signed Mohammed Ibn al-Malik.

Jean had no idea how to react to the letter. Was this someone's idea of a practical joke? If it was, why was it aimed at her? Or was this—and she held her breath— her first big break? She could see the screaming headlines in big, bold, black letters spread across the front page: YOUNG REPORTER FINDS MISSING TEN COMMANDMENTS! Why, it would be the most sensational scoop in the history of journalism.

Her soaring flight of fancy was quickly shot down by doubts. Suppose the letter was written by a nut? The

city, after all, was full of them. What if she wrote the
story up, and her newspaper printed it, and it turned
out to be a hoax? Her boss would fire her right off. And
if he didn't fire her, he would probably never allow her
to cover anything more than dull parties or weddings
for the rest of her career as a reporter.

Jean left the newspaper later that afternoon for
George's Coffee Shop where she was to meet Maximilian, Jessica, and Peter. After the usual bickering between Jessica and Peter, the children asked for Cokes
and Jean ordered a toasted cheese sandwich. As they
ate, Jean pulled out the letter from her purse and slipped
it to Maximilian.

Although Jean was twenty-one years old and Maximilian only twelve, the difference in their ages meant
little when it came to matters of hard fact. Jean recognized that Maximilian knew more than she did. To
her credit, Jean did not hesitate to ask for Maximilian's
help when she needed it, as she did now. He had never
let her down.

"What do you make of this?" Jean asked.

Maximilian read the letter with keen interest.

"Do you think there is anything to it?"

Maximilian said he was not sure. He did think that
Jean might want to meet Mr. al-Malik and judge for
herself.

Jean was willing to talk to Mr. al-Malik, providing
that Maximilian was present. Maximilian said he would
be glad to be there.

As soon as Maximilian set the letter down on the
table, Jessica and Peter both made a grab for it.

"Let go of it, you nerd!" Peter growled.

"Nuts to you, prune face!" Jessica replied.

Jean snatched the letter out of their hands before they ripped it to shreds. She ordered Maximilian to keep an eye on the pair while she went to the phone booth to call Mohammed Ibn al-Malik. She made an appointment for the next day at 4:30 P.M.

When Jessica and Peter learned that only Maximilian was invited to meet Mr. al-Malik, they complained loudly.

"You have no one to blame but yourselves," Jean said. "So long as you behave like children, you'll be treated like children; when you learn to behave like adults, you'll be treated like adults."

"It's all your fault!" Peter hissed.

"Shut your face, fat lips!" Jessica hit back.

"Jessica, how would you like to be the first person kicked into orbit?"

"Peter, if your IQ were any lower, you'd trip over it!"

"That does it! I've had it!" Jean threw up her hands. "Get your things, we're leaving this instant!"

"But, Jean!" Jessica and Peter pleaded.

Jean would not listen. She took them home.

The next day Maximilian and Jean were seated at a booth in George's Coffee Shop. At 4:30 P.M. precisely, an imposing figure dressed in a full-length white robe and wearing an Arab headdress entered. He glanced around the coffee shop like a king surveying his lowly vassals. He peered directly at their booth but then shifted his eyes elsewhere. The person he was looking for was not in Jean's booth.

Jean finally took matters into her own hands. She went up to Mr. al-Malik.

"Yes?" he said. He eyed her up and down as if she were an insect.

"Mr. al-Malik, sir. I am Jean Walker. I am the person to whom you spoke yesterday."

"You!" he said, making no effort to hide his disappointment. Mr. al-Malik had expected the newspaper to send an older, more experienced journalist. Instead, they sent a mere snip of a girl.

Nor was Mohammed Ibn al-Malik any more pleased to see Maximilian. Jean assured Mr. al-Malik that he was free to speak in front of Maximilian.

"I shall never understand your curious customs," Mr. al-Malik said huffily. "Where I come from, children are not permitted to be present when important matters are being discussed. Children should be home playing with their toys." He looked down at Maximilian and frowned.

Mr. al-Malik was not trying to win any popularity contests. He had already succeeded in offending Jean and Maximilian without even starting his interview. Jean decided to adopt a cool professional attitude. She simply ignored Mr. al-Malik's rudeness and unfriendly manner. She politely asked Mr. al-Malik to join them in their booth. He sat down. Jean then opened her reporter's notebook, poised her pencil as if to write, and looked at Mr. al-Malik expectantly.

Mr. al-Malik's manner abruptly changed. His sullen look vanished. "I have been unforgiveably rude to you as well as to your young friend," he said displaying a mouthful of pearly white teeth. "I have been such a poor host. I am thoroughly ashamed of myself. Is there anything I can get for you both before we begin? Are you hungry, or perhaps thirsty? You have but to speak."

Maximilian ordered a chocolate ice-cream soda. Jean scanned the menu and asked for a bacon and tomato sandwich on toast with a glass of orange juice. Mr. al-Malik ordered the same.

Mr. al-Malik began his story. "As I explained in my letter, Miss Walker, I know the whereabouts of the original two stone tablets given by Allah—or God as you say—to Moses on Mount Sinai. The tablets, or the Tablets of the Law, are inscribed with the Ten Commandments."

"Where are the Tablets of the Law now?" Jean asked.

"They are in my bank vault in Iraq. I am an Iraqi citizen, Miss Walker."

"Where were the Tablets of the Law found?"

"Also in Iraq. They were discovered in a small village called Hilla by farmers who were tilling their fields."

Jean looked up from her notebook. The story was beginning to interest her. "And how did the Tablets of the Law get to the village of Hilla?"

"For the answer to that question, Miss Walker, it is necessary to go back many, many centuries. The modern village of Hilla is near where the ancient city of Babylon once stood."

Jean looked up again. "Babylon was the capital of Babylonia, wasn't it?"

"Correct, Miss Walker."

"And, unless I am mistaken, Babylonia is approximately present-day Iraq."

"Again correct, Miss Walker. It all began over 2,500 years ago. The Babylonians under King Nebuchadnezzar conquered Jerusalem and destroyed the First Temple, also called Solomon's Temple. This occurred in the year 587 B.C. The Babylonians carried off all the First Temple's ceremonial objects, including the Tablets of the Law. They brought everything back to Babylon as war booty."

"What happened to the Tablets of the Law after they were taken to Babylon?"

"No one knows for sure, Miss Walker. They vanished from history. They vanished from history, that is, until the farmers of Hilla discovered them."

"And now you intend to sell the Tablets of the Law?"

"Allah forbid!" Mr. al-Malik said in horror. "That is the furthest thing from my mind. I could have sold the Tablets of the Law many times over had I so desired." He leaned forward. "Miss Walker, I am a religious man. As a good Mohammedan, I too revere Moses and of course the Ten Commandments. I have no wish to sell the Tablets of the Law. My true desire is to find a proper home for the Tablets of the Law. Should they be placed in Mecca, or in Rome, or returned to Jerusalem from whence they came, or should they be put on display in a public museum such as your wonderful Metropolitan Museum of Art? That is the question uppermost in my mind these days."

Mr. al-Malik then picked up his sandwich and took a bite. "Mmmm," he said hungrily. "This is the best bacon and tomato sandwich I've had in a long time."

40

"You then expect no money for the Tablets of the Law, Mr. al-Malik?"

"Allah be praised! I am a rich man. I have no need for money. None! Only as a matter of principle, I would like to be repaid for my expenses in acquiring the Tablets of the Law. That is all."

"And how much would that be?"

"The farmers who brought me the Tablets of the Law guessed how desperately I wanted those two stones. Those pirates held me up for $75,000. I had to pay them what they demanded. Then there are my travel expenses to Jerusalem, Mecca, Rome, and the United States." Mr. al-Malik smiled sweetly. "I should think $100,000 would cover it."

Alarm bells went off inside Jean's head. They clearly sounded *Danger!* Hadn't she recently almost been taken in by a man who claimed he had been captured by a band of little green men from outer space? Maximilian had saved her by spotting the story was a phony.

Jean shot Maximilian an inquiring glance. Maximilian shook his head ever so slightly to warn her that Mr. al-Malik was up to no good. Unfortunately, Mr. al-Malik also caught the meaning of their silent exchange.

Mr. al-Malik slipped out of the booth. In a voice dripping with venom, he declared, "Miss Walker, I am not accustomed to having my word doubted. I shall contact your superiors at the *New York Evening Star* and report your impudence." And with that Mohammed Ibn al-Malik stalked out of the coffee shop in a huff.

Jean's heart sank. Suppose Maximilian was wrong?

She was also shaken by Mr. al-Malik's threat to complain to her superiors at the newspaper.

"I wouldn't worry about him," Maximilian reassured Jean. "He won't give you any trouble." He then explained how he knew Mr. al-Malik was a fake.

Jean was relieved to learn the facts. "Just the same," she sighed, "it would have been nice if his story had been true."

Jean wondered when her big break would come.

How did Maximilian know Mr. al-Malik was a fraud?
(See page 122.)

6
. . . .
THE CASE OF
The Amateur
Coin Dealer

After the new police captain had complained about his appearance, Peter Wolfe promised to mend his ways. He had said he would make a sincere effort to improve his dress. However, Peter's good intentions vanished into thin air as he began to work on his new computer, CLAM 4. The computer became the most important thing in his life. He could think of nothing else.

Peter needed a place to build his computer. He wondered if he could use Benny the Onion's apartment. It was easy to persuade Benny to have a crime-solving computer right in his own home. Benny said he was fed up with being taken in by every crook and con artist roaming the streets of New York City. If a computer could tell him whether a deal was phony or not, it would save him money and aggravation.

Peter worked night and day on his computer. He sacrificed sleep and comfort. The day finally arrived when the computer was ready to be tested. He was convinced that this time his crime-solving computer would work. He would then become as famous in the history of criminal investigation as Sherlock Holmes. No. More famous!

Peter invited Benny and Maximilian to witness the CLAM 4 in action. Jessica invited herself.

Benny the Onion lived in what is known in New York City as a railroad flat. The apartment consisted of a series of small rooms laid along a long hallway, like in a railroad train. The room Benny allowed Peter to use was the last room down the dimly lit hallway. After everyone was settled in the room, Peter took off the bed sheet that had covered his new computer.

CLAM 4 was impressive. Peter's earlier computers had been piles of junk compared to this slick, modern, professional-looking computer.

Everyone wanted to know how CLAM 4 worked. Peter was happy to explain. Peter said the computer was made up of three basic parts. He pointed to the first part, which looked like a typewriter keyboard with several keys added. The computer operator sat at the keyboard and, by striking the proper keys, fed information and instructions into the computer.

The second part of the computer was a plain box. Peter explained the box contained a memory core and a set of instructions called a program. The memory core stored information. Unlike the human brain, however, the memory of the computer was perfect. The computer never forgot a thing. The program told the computer how to handle the information stored in the memory core. Peter said the hardest part of making his computer work was designing the right program.

Peter pointed to the third part of the computer. It resembled a television screen. Peter called the screen a computer readout terminal or a monitor. The screen displayed information fed into the computer, what questions you asked, and finally the answers to your questions.

"Isn't she a beauty?" Peter beamed. Benny and Maximilian agreed Peter had every reason to feel proud.

Only Jessica had reservations. "It looks nice," she said, "but will it work? For all we know, it may be a pile of useless junk." She sniffed.

"Jessica, you still have thirty-two teeth. How would you like to try for none?"

"You should leave your brain to science, Peter. Maybe they can find a cure for it."

"Now, now, kids," Benny said soothingly.

Peter ignored Jessica. "My theory is that every crime has one or more logical flaws. Find these logical flaws, and the crime is as good as solved."

"That's absurd," Maximilian objected. "All logic can do is to uncover inconsistencies where all the parts are supplied and none is missing. In a crime, something is missing. That's why you call it a mystery."

"I must disagree with you," Peter said. "What is important in solving crimes is not the facts, but how the facts hang together. Do the facts support each other? Do the facts contradict one another? These are the questions a true detective asks."

"It's none of my business, and I hate to butt in, but I think you both have a point," Jessica said, flicking her pigtails back.

"You're right," Peter said. "It is none of your business—so butt out!"

Peter said he could prove it was logic and not mere facts. He knew that Benny the Onion was considering a new business. Peter suggested they use the CLAM 4 to find out if the business was an honest one or not.

"What kind of business are you thinking of going into?" Maximilian asked.

Benny announced dramatically, "I'm going to become a dealer in ancient coins."

Benny the Onion had dreamed up some pretty wild schemes, but even Maximilian was astonished by this one.

"Do you mind if I ask you a question, Benny?" Maximilian asked.

"Not at all. Ask, ask."

"You won't get angry at me, will you?"

"No. Why should I?"

"What do you know about ancient coins?"

"What do I know about ancient coins!" Benny gagged. Then he remembered his promise not to get angry. "What's there to know?" he said grandly.

"It's a complicated subject. It takes years to become an expert on ancient coins. You'll be clobbered!"

"There you go again! Sometimes I worry about you, Maximilian. You know what your trouble is? You have a suspicious nature. And do you know why you have a suspicious nature? It's because you hang around the Mid-Manhattan Precinct House. You think the world is full of crooks. Trust me, my boy, I know what I'm doing. I'm no amateur."

"But Benny . . ." Maximilian tried to get in a word.

"Tut, tut! What's the big deal? I'm aware that people say I don't have much upstairs, but even I can read dates."

"Read dates?"

"You heard me."

Benny went to another room and returned carrying three coins. The coins were all identical.

"This is an ancient Roman coin called the denarius. Look at the bottom of the coin. See there. . . ." Benny pointed to CLXXX B.C. "That means 180 B.C."

Maximilian examined the three coins. "I hope you didn't pay too much money for these."

"To tell the truth, I didn't have enough to pay for the coins. The man who sold them to me asked $150 for all three. I gave him a deposit of $15. It was all I had."

"Benny, I advise you not to sell the coins. If you try to pass them off as genuine, you could get yourself into real trouble."

"There you go again! Always suspicious. Always seeing criminals hiding in every dark corner."

Peter repeated his suggestion that they put his computer to work to find out if the coins were genuine or not.

"Terrific idea!" Benny said.

Peter handed Benny a long questionnaire. After the questionnaire had been filled out, Peter sat down at the keyboard and began to feed information from the questionnaire into the computer. Speedy, Peter was not. The minutes dragged on.

Benny fidgeted impatiently. "How long is this going to take?"

"Soon, soon," Peter said.

"By the time his computer gets going, a real criminal would have died of old age," Jessica said sarcastically.

"Who asked for your opinion?" Peter looked up from the keyboard with disgust. "Isn't there enough stupidity in the world already?"

Peter was so rattled his hand accidentally brushed the wrong key. The information already entered into the computer was immediately wiped out. "See what you made me do!" he whined. "Now I have to start all over again."

Everyone groaned. Finally, after what seemed like an eternity, the task was completed.

Peter looked up at the display screen, eyes filled with hope. It was the moment of truth. He sucked in his breath and pushed a button. The computer clicked and hummed but nothing showed on the screen, except for some meaningless blips. Then the screen went dark. Peter stared at the blank screen, tears streaming down his cheeks. CLAM 4 was a failure.

"Don't you have another button you can press?" Benny asked hopefully. Peter did not respond. He probably hadn't even heard what Benny had said. He stared like a zombie at the blank screen, dead to anything but his bitter disappointment.

Jessica was about to make some nasty remark about the computer, but Maximilian put his finger to his lips to caution her to be silent. Peter was miserable enough.

Benny still did not know whether his coins were fake or not. It was up to Maximilian to prove it one way or the other.

There was no need for Maximilian to go into his customary concentration routine. He had figured the case out already. He wrote in his memo book and showed it to Benny.

Benny sputtered. "Why the dirty crook! Wait until I get my hands on him!"

Benny dashed out of the apartment to find the man who had sold him the fake coins.

Why were the coins fake?
(See page 123.)

7

. . . .

THE CASE OF
Double Trouble

Nothing could keep Peter down for long. He had about as much bounce as someone on a pogo stick. He assured Benny the Onion the problem with his computer was a minor one. He dismissed the difficulty with a wave of his hand and a brave smile. "All I have to do," he said brimming with confidence, "is to replace the 4K chips with 64K chips."

"Huh?" Benny said.

"Sorry. I didn't mean to use technical language." Peter scratched his chin and organized his thoughts like a college professor about to lecture his students.

"A chip is the basic building block of the computer. You could compare it to a brain cell. Just as the brain is a network of brain cells, a computer is a network of chips."

"What's a chip?"

"A chip is a tiny wafer of thinly sliced silicon. Silicon is the basic element in sand."

"I see," Benny said weakly.

"The purpose of the chip is to store information. Chips are getting smaller while their capacity for storing information is getting larger. The latest generation of chips is called the 64K chip. This means the chip can store about 64,000 bits of information. My present computer uses the older 4K chips. The 4K chip can store only about 4,000 bits of information. The 64K chip holds up to sixteen times more information than the 4K chip."

Peter paused. "Follow me so far?"

Benny could hear his voice saying yes, but his brain saying no.

"A computer cannot create information out of nothing. In other words, you get out of a computer only what you put into it. Since you are able to put more information into a computer using 64K chips than into one using 4K chips, the 64K chip computer is 'smarter' than a 4K chip computer. You can ask a 64K chip computer more questions and get better and more answers."

Peter was grateful for the chance to talk about his ideas, even if Benny did not fully understand them.

"All I have to do is replace my present 4K chips with 64K chips, and I guarantee you I'll have a computer that will solve crimes. It's that simple."

Peter's optimism quickly faded. Building computers was an expensive hobby. Where was he going to get enough money to buy 64K chips?

Benny the Onion told Peter not to worry. The Canal

Street area was the main district in New York City for surplus electronic parts. If 64K chips were available anywhere, and at a low price, they would be found here. Benny boasted that he knew the Canal Street area like the back of his hand.

They went down to Canal Street the following Saturday. They tried a dozen stores. No one had the 64K chips. The store owners said the 64K chips were only recently developed. The chips were too new to be found in surplus electronic stores.

They ran into a man just as they were about to give up. The man said he could get them all the 64K chips they wanted. The price he mentioned was unbelievably low. Peter wondered how he could offer the 64K chips at that price. Peter brushed his suspicions aside. It wasn't his problem. He wanted those chips badly. A deal was quickly made.

What added to Peter's suspicion was the man's eyes. They bulged from his head as if they were about to pop out. They also never stood still. They darted about as if the man feared someone or something was after him. It was impossible to look at those eyes for long without getting nervous.

After the deal was made, the man invited Benny and Peter to join him in a snack. Peter had a chocolate milk shake, Benny a cup of coffee, and the man a bowl of steaming lamb stew. The man promised to deliver the chips to Benny's home later in the day. "It is now 4:15 P.M.," the man said, looking at his watch. "I can be there in an hour. Is that all right with you?" Benny and Peter said that would be fine.

The man delivered the 64K chips exactly as promised.

The chips were not the usual secondhand electronic parts one found on Canal Street. These chips were brand new and still in their original boxes. Peter whistled a happy tune as he removed the chips from their boxes. He was confident he could now build a crime-solving computer.

Maximilian read a recent story in the newspaper about an unusual robbery. Thieves had broken into a warehouse of a computer manufacturer on Church Street off Canal Street. The thieves were highly selective. They left the larger electronic parts behind and took only the chips.

The thieves knew something about electronics. Chips are used in the manufacture of all computers, video games, calculators, and similar electronic devices. Most manufacturers use the same, interchangeable chips. The chips could therefore be disposed of easily.

Peter was too busy with his own computer to be aware of the robbery. He was astonished when Maximilian told him thieves had stolen chips. He was dismayed to learn the chips were of the 64K variety. Peter knew his duty. He immediately contacted Detective Walker and told him about the 64K chips he had bought.

Peter and Benny furnished Detective Walker with a description of the man who sold them the chips. Store owners on Canal Street were asked to contact the police if anyone answering the description tried to sell them 64K chips.

A call came in for Detective Walker. It was a store owner. A man matching the description and offering to sell 64K chips was now in his store. Detective Walker asked the store owner to stall the man until he could get there. Unfortunately, while the store owner did his best, the man grew suspicious and fled. Detective Walker returned to his car and cruised the neighborhood. He spotted the suspect ten minutes later entering a Chinese restaurant.

Detective Walker identified himself as a police officer. The man admitted he was trying to sell 64K chips. He declared he had no idea the chips were stolen, however. He said his name was Lem Huggins.

"Where did you say you got the 64K chips, Mr. Huggins?"

"I bought them from a man."

"What was the man's name?"

"I don't know. He approached me and asked if I wanted to buy 64K chips. I said yes. I paid him. That's all there was to it. I never saw the man before, and I haven't seen him since."

"You're sure you don't know who the man was, Mr. Huggins?"

"Look, Detective Walker, I really would like to cooperate with the police, honest. But I've told you everything I know."

Detective Walker stared, fascinated by those bulging eyes darting nervously about.

Detective Walker than asked Lem Huggins to accompany him to the warehouse from which the chips had been stolen. The warehouse was nearby.

When the elevator operator of the warehouse saw Lem Huggins, he exploded. "That's the guy, officer! That's the guy who hit me over the head. Let me take a crack at him, the rat! Just one little punch!"

The elevator operator would have done so had not Detective Walker stopped him.

"Are you sure this is the man who hit you over the head?"

"Of course I'm sure! How could I forget those pop eyes?"

The elevator operator made another lunge at Lem Huggins. It was all Detective Walker could do to restrain him. Detective Walker then asked the elevator operator to describe what happened.

"I was reading a newspaper in my elevator on the day of the robbery, which was a Saturday, when this guy came into the building. He asked me what time it was. I told him. The time was 3:30 P.M. Then the next thing I know, I wake up in the hospital with a head that feels like someone is using it for bongo drums."

"Are you sure of the time?"

"Positively! Why would I make it up?"

"You're a liar!" Lem Huggins said angrily, his eyes popping even more than usual. "I don't have to put up with this, you know. Wait until you hear from my lawyer!"

"Where do you get off threatening me?" The elevator operator flew into a rage. "Give me a break, officer. Can't I have just one little crack at him? Huh? *Please!*"

"So long as you two are arguing with each other we're not going to get anywhere. Take it easy. Calm down."

Detective Walker then asked Lem Huggins where he was on the day and time in question.

"I was having my tooth filled at my dentist's on

Saturday. I got to his office at 3:30 P.M. and left at 4:30 P.M."

He searched his wallet until he found what he was looking for. It was a dentist's card. Lem Huggins extended the card to Detective Walker. "Talk to him if you like. His office is down the street."

Detective Walker checked with the dentist. The dentist verified Lem Huggins's story.

"See, officer, I told you I'm innocent." Lem Huggins smirked. "A person can't be in two places at the same time, now, can he? Someone else must have hit the elevator operator over the head. It sure wasn't me."

The elevator operator was stunned. He could not believe what was happening. He was positive this was the man. His mouth opened slowly, words were forming in his brain, but nothing came out. How do you argue with the facts?

Detective Walker returned to the precinct house. He was stuck. Was there some detail he had overlooked? Was there some question he had failed to ask? Was there some moment of time not accounted for? He asked himself these questions again and again over the next few days. He reluctantly concluded he could not spend any more time on the case.

In the past, Detective Walker would not have given up so soon. Things were different now. Because of cuts in the city budget, the precinct house was short five detectives. The number of cases assigned to Detective Walker was staggering. He was handed three new cases just that morning. Sometimes Detective Walker had the feeling he was on the losing side. The criminals were able to commit crimes faster than the police were able to solve them.

As Detective Walker was about to place the file on the 64K chip case in the INACTIVE file, Maximilian asked if he could look at it. Detective Walker handed the file to him.

Maximilian found a quiet corner in the precinct house, unwrapped a chocolate bar, and settled down to read the case.

One detail caught his attention and separated itself from the rest. What was the significance of this detail? He concentrated so hard, his brow knit and his eyes narrowed to slits. Then it came to him.

Maximilian told Detective Walker what he had uncovered in reading the file. Detective Walker was not impressed. "That's all very well and good, and I appreciate your pointing it out. However, how can one person be in two places at the same time?"

"Exactly!" Maximilian exclaimed. He then scribbled furiously in his memo book and showed it to Detective Walker.

Detective Walker still looked doubtful. "Are you sure?" he asked Maximilian.

"It is the only possible way to explain all the facts."

Detective Walker agreed to check it out, but only because Maximilian seemed to be so positive.

Detective Walker soon returned, not with one prisoner, but with two. The pair made people gasp. Were they seeing things? The two men dressed alike, spoke alike, acted alike, and looked alike—down to their bulging eyes. The names of the prisoners were Lem and Clem Huggins. They were identical twins.

The two brothers loudly protested their innocence. Detective Walker was not paying attention. He simply showed them Maximilian's memo book. They read the memo book and stopped protesting. What was the use? They knew they were caught.

"That kid is a great detective," one of the brothers said in sincere admiration. But whether it was Lem Huggins or Clem Huggins who spoke, Maximilian could not say, because he could not tell them apart. He blushed a deep red nonetheless. A compliment was a compliment.

"This reminds me of a riddle," Detective Walker spoke up. "What close relatives do computer chips have?"

"I don't know," one brother said.

"What?" the other brother asked.

"Transisters."

How did Maximilian know the thieves were twins? (See page 124.)

8

· · · · · · · ·

THE CASE OF

Professor Marvello
the Great

Jean's job as a cub reporter on the *New York Evening
Star* was getting her down. If she didn't get away soon,
she would scream. Even a weekend away from the city
would help.

Detective Walker suggested they try Big Mountain
Ridge in upstate New York for a weekend of skiing. The
last time they were there they had a wonderful time.
Perhaps Maximilian would come along, as he did before.

"But how will we get to Big Mountain Ridge?" Jean
worried. "My broken-down car won't make the trip."

"We can always take the bus," Detective Walker said.

Maximilian was excited about going on another ski
trip with Jean and Detective Walker.

Their bus was to leave from Port Authority Bus Terminal on 42 Street and Eighth Avenue. The area around the terminal was one of the grimiest in the city. For years people had been talking about cleaning it up. Nothing ever came of it.

They couldn't wait for the bus to leave. The bus finally edged out of the terminal. It emerged onto the streets, but soon went into a long tunnel, the Lincoln Tunnel. The bus came into the open again, finally. They saw a sign saying Welcome to New Jersey.

The landscape changed rapidly. The city vanished and was replaced by suburbs. The suburbs gave out. They were soon in the country. They leaned back in their seats and enjoyed the passing scenery.

Three hours later the bus pulled into the grounds of Big Mountain Ridge. As they stepped off the bus, they were hit by a blast of fresh air. People who live in the city tend to forget how delicious fresh air can smell. They breathed in long and deep. Unfortunately, the fresh air also made Maximilian crave a chocolate bar.

They registered in the main lodge, unpacked, and rented ski equipment. They then went to the dining room for lunch. The lodge had a reputation for good food. The reputation was well deserved. Lunch was excellent.

They skied all afternoon. Maximilian did very well. Having only skied once before, he was a bit shaky on his feet at first. However, as the afternoon wore on, Maximilian proved to be a natural skier. Detective Walker could barely keep up with him.

They were all to have dinner at six o'clock. Jean had not as yet returned from the ski slopes. Detective Walker was beginning to worry. She finally turned up at 6:30 P.M., holding hands with a young man. His name was Dan Archer. Dan was a third-year law student. Would her father mind if Dan joined them at dinner? Detective Walker said Dan was more than welcome.

Jean and Dan hardly touched their food. They were too busy gazing into each other's eyes. It was obvious even to Maximilian, who knew little about such matters, that they were smitten with each other. There was no point in trying to talk to them. They were interested only in each other.

After dinner Jean and Dan drifted off somewhere together. Detective Walker and Maximilian had planned on taking in a show in the lodge theater. The main attraction was Professor Marvello the Great, a famous hypnotist.

Professor Marvello the Great appeared on stage dressed in a black cape, tuxedo, and top hat. He introduced his assistant, a pretty young woman named Miss Lee. Miss Lee placed two empty milk cases on the stage. Professor Marvello the Great then dangled a shiny pocket watch before Miss Lee and repeated, "You are getting sleepy; you are getting sleepy." Miss Lee's eyelids drooped and then shut. She was in a deep trance. Professor Marvello said over and over again, "Your body is getting stiff; your body is getting stiff." Miss Lee's body grew more and more rigid.

Professor Marvello the Great now invited two men from the audience to come up on stage. He asked the two men to lift the rigid Miss Lee and place her across the two milk boxes so that her head rested on one box, her feet on the other. They had no trouble lifting the tiny Miss Lee. Professor Marvello the Great then invited the two men to sit on Miss Lee's stomach. They hesitated. How could this frail woman's body support the weight of two grown men? Professor Marvello the Great insisted. The two men sat down on the small rigid body as if they were sitting down on eggs. They were amazed because her body did not yield an inch. They even lifted their feet off the floor so their entire weight could rest on Miss Lee's body, supported as it was by only two milk boxes. Her body held like a steel bar. The audience roared its approval.

For his next demonstration, Professor Marvello the Great asked for a single volunteer from the audience. A woman came up on stage. Professor Marvello the Great hypnotized her, again by dangling a watch in front of her eyes. When she was fully hypnotized, he suggested that she was hungry and that a tomato would taste delicious. However, instead of giving her a tomato, he substituted a large onion. The woman bit into the onion and munched happily on it as if it were the sweetest of tomatoes. When she had finished every bit of the onion, Professor Marvello the Great snapped his fingers and she awoke. Immediately tears gushed from the woman's eyes as if someone had opened a faucet. She honked helplessly into a handkerchief. She also complained of an awful oniony taste in her mouth and a peculiar feeling in her stomach. Again, the audience enjoyed the act hugely.

Next, Professor Marvello the Great asked if anyone in the audience wanted to give up smoking. Dozens of hands shot up. Apparently there were a lot of people who wanted to quit. One man was selected. He came up on stage and was put into a trance as the others had been. After determining that the man was fully asleep, Professor Marvello the Great told him that whenever he puffed on a cigarette his mouth would feel as if it were on fire. Professor Marvello the Great then snapped his fingers and the man awoke.

The man left the stage and went back to his table. He had no idea what had happened while he was on the stage. He wondered why the audience was staring at him. The man felt nervous and lit up a cigarette. He took one puff, gagged, clutched his throat, and screamed, "Help! My mouth is on fire! Help! My mouth is on fire!" He grabbed a pitcher of water from a passing waiter and gulped it all down. The audience rocked with laughter.

Professor Marvello the Great concluded his act by warning the audience not to regard hypnosis as a mere trick or as a toy. Hypnosis was a powerful force which only skilled professionals could handle safely.

The telephone woke Detective Walker early the next morning. It was the manager of the lodge. The manager knew that Detective Walker was a member of the New York City Police Department. He apologized for disturbing Detective Walker so early, but would he be good enough to come to the front desk. The manager said the matter was urgent. Detective Walker wiped the sleep from his eyes and got dressed.

As he approached the front desk, he heard the lodge manager arguing with Miss Lee.

"What seems to be the problem?" Detective Walker asked.

"I caught this woman trying to walk off with the lodge's cashbox."

"That's a lie!" the woman hissed.

"What's in the cashbox?"

"All the change from our pinball and electronic games. The cashbox has about $10,000 in it. It beats me, though, how this tiny lady moved it all by herself. I can hardly budge it."

"There, you see, officer! It's a lie. How could I lift anything that heavy?"

Looking at the tiny lady in front of him, Detective Walker also found it hard to believe.

"Are you going to take that tramp's word over mine?" the manager said in a huff.

"What did you call me, you miserable worm you?" Miss Lee sprang at the manager like a tiger. She grabbed him by the seat of his pants, and with one effortless sweep, lifted him straight over her head as if he were a feather.

"Help!" the manager screamed in panic.

"Set him down!" Detective Walker commanded.

Miss Lee let the manager drop to the floor. He landed with a dull thud on his backside.

Detective Walker helped the poor man up. His breath had been knocked out of him but he was otherwise unhurt. "Some weak little lady!" The manager swore under his breath.

Detective Walker was surprised by her strength. Surprise soon gave way to suspicion. Maybe the lodge manager was telling the truth. This little lady was capable of amazing feats of strength. She could have walked off with the cashbox if she had wanted to.

A crowd began to gather. Detective Walker thought it best to continue the investigation in the privacy of the manager's office. Once inside the manager's office, Detective Walker contacted the local chief of police. He also called Maximilian and Professor Marvello the Great. They all arrived within minutes.

The local chief of police knew Detective Walker. They had met the last time Detective Walker was at Big Mountain Ridge. He also remembered Maximilian.

Detective Walker told the chief of police what he had learned about the case up to this point.

"Professor Marvello," Miss Lee pleaded, "you've got to help me. Tell the police that I'm innocent. Please?"

Professor Marvello the Great shook his head sadly. "I know how important you are to my act. You would be hard to replace. But I cannot lie. Besides, you've only been with me for a week. I know next to nothing about you."

"Is there any special reason why she is hard to replace?" the local police chief asked.

"My act requires an assistant of great strength. One of my big tricks is to have Miss Lee stretched across two milk boxes while two men sit on her stomach."

"I know," Detective Walker interrupted. "I saw your act last night. I enjoyed it very much."

"Thank you, Detective Walker. I appreciate that. Now,

the public thinks the trick is a matter of hypnosis. I hope that what I am about to say won't get beyond these four walls, but hypnosis has nothing to do with this particular feat. It is actually a question of strength. Miss Lee locks her back in place with her powerful stomach muscles. She then can support unbelievable weights."

"Not a word the Professor is saying is true!" Miss Lee protested. "He is an evil man. He put me into a deep trance, and when I was helpless, ordered me to steal the cashbox."

"Ridiculous!" Professor Marvello the Great dismissed the idea.

"Don't anyone listen to him. You've seen his act. You've seen the incredible things he can do with people. He can work people like puppets. He can make them do anything he wants."

Miss Lee's words set off a chain reaction in Maximilian's brain. What had he read about hypnotism? It was not necessary to go into his concentration routine. The facts he needed were fresh in his mind, and he had no special difficulty in recalling them.

Maximilian wrote in his memo book and passed it to Detective Walker. Detective Walker read the memo book with pleasure. He then showed it to the local chief of police.

The local police chief was impressed. He told Maximilian how much he admired his firm grasp of police matters. Maximilian's face turned beet-red.

Miss Lee would not accept defeat. "Professor Marvello the Great made me do it. He put me into a trance. He made my mind do his bidding. I was as helpless as a sleepwalker."

"That reminds me of a riddle," Detective Walker said. "Why did the sleepwalker put carfare in his pajamas?"

"I don't know," Miss Lee said. "Why?"

"In case he walked in his sleep, he could take the bus back home."

Everyone laughed except Miss Lee. She gave Detective Walker a look that needed washing.

How did Maximilian know Miss Lee was lying?
(See page 126.)

9

. . . .

THE CASE OF
The Missing Gag File

If, as they say, "April showers bring May flowers," there ought to be more than the usual number of flowers in May. April was turning out to be one of the wettest in history. The rain had been especially heavy over the last few days. Everyone had found a way of coping with the rain. Detective Walker used the time to whittle down the mountain of paperwork that had been piling up on his desk.

The phone rang. Detective Walker picked it up. "Yes?" he said.

"I wish to report a robbery." The caller's voice broke.

"Was anyone hurt in the robbery?"

"No."

"What is your name, please?"

"Howie Dixon."

Detective Walker sat up straight. "Not *the* Howie Dixon who used to be in television?"

"The one and same. It's nice to know people still remember me."

"Mr. Dixon, I used to watch your television shows all the time. That must have been in the fifties. Gosh, that was a long time ago."

"Well, you don't have to rub it in!"

"Sorry. I didn't mean to offend you."

"That's all right."

"I not only remember you, Mr. Dixon, but you'd be surprised how popular you still are with young people who weren't even alive when you were on the air. I have a young friend who is a great fan of yours. He watches all your old reruns on TV."

"Really?" Howie Dixon was flattered. "What's the young man's name?"

"Maximilian Augustus Adams."

"Maximilian sounds like an intelligent lad. He should go far. You can tell Maximilian that I'd like nothing better than to shake his hand one day."

"Really? That's wonderful of you. I'll be sure to tell him. Now, I will need more details about the robbery. Exactly what was stolen?"

"My gag file."

There was silence as Detective Walker considered Howie Dixon's words. "I have to confess," Detective Walker finally admitted, "I don't know what a gag file is."

"You don't know what a gag file is!" Howie Dixon sucked in his breath. "Sorry, I keep forgetting not everyone is in show business. A gag file is a collection of jokes. No, it is more than a collection of jokes. A gag file is the very lifeblood of a comedian's career. It is every joke he has ever heard, carefully and lovingly preserved. It is years of collecting jokes from books, from other comedians, from people."

"I thought comedians made up their own jokes."

"That's a laugh! My friend, believe me when I tell you there are no new jokes under the sun. There are only old jokes. Sure, a joke can be changed around a bit to make it fit the comedian or the situation or the times, but underneath it all it is still the same old joke."

"I didn't know that."

"It took me over twenty-five years of steady collecting to build up my gag file. It also took hundreds and hundreds of hours to index and cross-index the jokes so that I could quickly find a joke on any subject I happened to need. Now that my gag file is missing, I'm as good as finished!"

"Was the gag file insured?"

"I'm afraid not."

"Was anything else taken in the robbery?"

"I don't think so."

"Is it all right if I come right over?"

"That would be inconvenient. Can you make it this evening?"

"How does eight o'clock sound?"

"That sounds fine. And, if your young friend Maximilian is free and is brave enough to come out in rainy weather like this, by all means bring him along."

70

Detective Walker took Howie Dixon's address and said he would be there. Maximilian was thrilled at the opportunity to meet one of the great comedians of all time.

The house was a beautiful brownstone on a quiet street on the Upper East Side. Howie Dixon lived on the ground floor. Detective Walker rang the bell. Howie Dixon answered the door. He smiled warmly at his two guests until he noticed their wet clothing.

"Don't you dare come in!" he barked. "You're all dripping wet. Leave your wet things out in the hall. And be sure you wipe your feet dry before you come in."

He checked his visitors over carefully before they were allowed to enter. It was soon clear why Howie Dixon was so fussy. Almost everything in the apartment was pure white. The walls were white, as were the rugs, the curtains, the furniture, the lamps. The only things in the room not white were the many photographs on the wall. The photographs showed Howie Dixon with the stars he had worked with. The photographs were lovingly dedicated to Howie Dixon.

Howie Dixon noticed Maximilian's keen interest in the photographs.

"Yes, kid"—Howie Dixon draped his arm over Maximilian's shoulder—"I've been around for a long time. I've worked with the best. I played vaudeville. Many a time I had top billing at the Palace. Then I went into the movies. When television came along, I worked with Milton Berle, Jack Benny, Sid Caesar, Jackie Gleason. You name them, I've worked with them."

"Weren't you at one time partners with Fred Lewis?" Maximilian asked.

The color drained from Howie Dixon's face. "Don't you dare mention that name in my presence again, young man!" he said, barely able to restrain his anger.

Too late Maximilian remembered. Howie Dixon and Fred Lewis had once been partners. They starred in one of the first of the big comedy programs on television. They had a bitter quarrel and split up. Each got his own show. They soon began to compete for sponsors, time slots, ratings. Occasionally, one would make an unflattering remark about the other on the air. It always brought laughs. Not wishing to throw perfectly good laughs away, they increased the number of occasions in which they took potshots at each other. To get still bigger laughs, their attacks on each other grew more vicious. Their animosity soon spilled over into real life. Hardly a week went by without some gossip columnist's mentioning their squabbles. Their feud became famous in the history of show business.

"Where was the missing gag file kept, Mr. Dixon?" Detective Walker asked, resuming his questioning.

Howard Dixon led them to the library. This room, like the others, was also spotless white. Even the books on the shelves were covered with white paper to keep the color of the room uniform.

Howard Dixon pointed to a stand in the center of the library. "The gag file stood on top of that."

"What did the gag file look like?"

"It looked like a card catalog in a library. It had thirty drawers, six across and five high. All told, there were about sixty thousand cards in the file."

"Was the gag file heavy?"

"It would have taken at least two men to lift it."

Detective Walker inspected the windows in the library. A pane had been smashed. The pane was now covered with a piece of cardboard to keep the rain out.

"What do you think happened, Mr. Dixon?"

Howie Dixon thought for a moment before he spoke. "I believe the thieves broke the window from the outside, reached through, and opened the latch. They then entered the library and walked off with my gag file."

The rug around the window was free of glass and was spotless. Detective Walker peered through the broken pane. He could see pieces of glass on the ground outside. A path led from the window to the sidewalk.

"When was the last time you saw the gag file?"

"About seven thirty last night."

"When did you find the gag file missing?"

"Early this morning."

"Sounds like the gag file was stolen sometime during the night while you were asleep."

"That would explain why I didn't hear the thieves break the windowpane and walk off with my gag file."

Then Howie Dixon dropped a bombshell. He said he knew who had stolen the gag file. "It was Fred Lewis," he said. "Fred Lewis hated me from the old days. He still hates me. He hates me even more now that I am making a comeback, especially among young people."

"I can't believe Fred Lewis would stoop to such a thing." Detective Walker offered the opinion.

"Oh, no?" You don't know that fink the way I do. He

would do anything to stop me. I couldn't make a comeback without my gag file. He knew that. That's why he stole it. Oh, I don't mean he took my gag file in person. He is along in years now—ahem—just like me. He must have hired a couple of goons to do his dirty work."

Howie Dixon's words set off a chain reaction in Maximilian's brain. His brow creased and his eyes narrowed to mere slits as he concentrated. His expression soon relaxed, however. He had found the solution to the mystery. Maximilian wrote in his memo book and passed it to Detective Walker.

Detective Walker smiled and nodded in approval after he read. "Mr. Dixon," he said, "Maximilian has shown me why your story does not stand up. Fred Lewis did not steal your gag file."

"Who did then?"

"You!"

"If that's your idea of a joke, you've just laid an egg."

"I'm dead serious. It was you who took the gag file. There was no robbery."

"Where's your proof?"

"Right here." Detective Walker handed Maximilian's memo book to Howie Dixon.

Howie Dixon read what Maximilian had written. He shrugged his shoulders. "Okay, you guys win. Can't say I didn't try, though. Smart boy, Maximilian. Come here, young man, let me shake your hand."

Maximilian blushed.

"That reminds me of a riddle," Detective Walker said. "What has wings, lays eggs, and cracks jokes?"

"I don't know," Howie Dixon said. "What?"

"A comedi-hen!"

"Not bad, not bad," Howie Dixon said. He quickly found pencil and paper and wrote down the riddle. "That goes into my gag file." He chuckled.

How did Maximilian know the gag file was not stolen?
(See page 127.)

10

. . . .

THE CASE OF
The Friendly Pythons

Detective Walker and Jean promised to take Maximilian, Peter, and Jessica to the Bronx Zoo just as soon as the weather turned pleasant. That Sunday was a glorious spring day, perfect for the zoo. Detective Walker and the children took the subway. Jean and Dan went separately in Dan's car. They were all to meet at the East 180 Street zoo entrance of the Bronx Zoo.

Detective Walker and the children were the first to arrive. Jean and Dan showed up a few minutes later.

Peter and Jessica had not met Dan before. Jean introduced them. Maximilian had already met Dan on the ski trip up at Big Mountain Ridge.

Jessica developed an immediate crush on Dan. She thought he was a dream. She hoped that when she grew up she would have a boyfriend as handsome.

Life had changed a good deal for Jean since she met Dan. Life for her now had a different meaning, a richer purpose. In other words, Jean was in love. Jean and Dan would officially announce their engagement soon.

The only zoo the children had seen before was the small zoo in Central Park. The Bronx Zoo was very different. The animals in the Central Park Zoo were kept in small, cramped cages. The animals in the Bronx Zoo, on the other hand, were allowed to roam over large areas surrounded by moats rather than bars. Every effort was made to set the animals in as natural an environment as possible. One might think the animals would try to jump across the moats and escape. But why should they? They had everything they wanted and needed right where they were. They were content to stay put. A few of the older areas of the Bronx Zoo still had barred cages. These were rapidly being replaced.

After wandering over the spacious grounds, Detective Walker looked for a place to rest. Besides, it was time for lunch. The group found a cafeteria where one could enjoy food out-of-doors under large umbrellas.

Everyone was hungry and dug in. Everyone, that is, except Jean and Dan. They were more interested in holding hands and in gazing dreamily into each other's eyes. Jessica sighed. She thought love was grand.

As nearly always happened when Peter and Maximilian were together, they discussed their favorite theory of how crimes are solved. Maximilian thought it was through facts; Peter thought it was through logic.

After listening to their conversation, Jessica flicked

back her pigtails and offered her opinion. "I personally think both of you are right."

Peter scowled. "Who asked you, mush mouth?"

"Peter, why don't you let your hair grow—right over your face."

Jean warned, "Am I going to have trouble with you two again? One more peep out of you both, just one, and it's back home for you both."

Peter and Jessica stopped.

Maximilian hoped he could draw Dan into the discussion. He must have some ideas on the subject. After all, Dan was a third-year law student.

Dan paused to collect his thoughts. "Jessica thinks both of you are right. I am of the opinion that both of you are wrong."

"But how can that be?" Maximilian protested. "Impossible!" Peter added.

"The trouble is that both of you think of crime solely as a police matter. Crime is as much a legal matter."

"What's the difference?" Maximilian wanted to know.

"Yes, what's the difference?" Peter echoed.

"The difference is that when a criminal is arrested for a crime or is booked for a crime, he is only suspected of having committed a crime. He has not been proven guilty of the crime. Proof of guilt is established only in a court of law."

Maximilian was not convinced. "But don't you prove guilt on the basis of facts? And isn't it the police who provide the facts?"

"The problem is that we don't always have *all* the

facts. Even with the best police work, the facts may be challenged. The facts may be incomplete, missing, or even contradictory. They have to be interpreted, argued, sifted. This is what lawyers, judges, and juries do."

"But how about logic?" Peter spoke up.

"Logic is fine and it has its place. The trouble is that logic deals in absolutes—yes or no, black or white. In real life and in the courts, things are seldom yes or no. They're mostly maybe, mostly shades of gray."

Detective Walker had been following Dan's speech with increasing irritation. He finally had to speak. "You already sound like a lawyer, Dan. If I arrest someone, I don't arrest him because I *think* he is guilty, but because I *know* it."

"And you could be wrong," Dan said.

"Not as often as some judges and lawyers would think. When I arrest a punk with a long record for mugging people, and some bleeding-heart judge or some fast-talking lawyer gets him off with a slight slap on the wrist, I get mad—I get plenty mad."

"Even a criminal is entitled to rights," Dan said with conviction.

"How about the victims? The way the system now operates, the criminal has more rights than the victim. I don't call that justice. Do you?" asked Detective Walker.

"Everyone is entitled to equal protection under the law." Dan held his ground.

"I'd like to see you explain that to an old woman who has been knocked down by a purse snatcher and had her last five dollars stolen. Then I'd like to see you argue with the rat that knocked her down, and tell him he should stop doing it because he is interfering with another person's civil rights. He'll laugh at you and then spit in your eye."

Jean was horrified by the direction the discussion was taking. She was upset because her father and Dan were on opposite sides of important questions. "It's too beautiful a day to settle all the world's problems," she said, smiling her prettiest smile. "I wonder what that is over there." She pointed to a building in the distance.

Jessica checked the zoo map. It was the reptile house.

"You mean where they have the snakes!" Jean shuddered.

Jessica could not understand why people disliked snakes. She thought they were beautiful, clean, and very interesting. She even had a pet snake once, until her mother made her get rid of it.

The group made their way to the reptile house. They had to practically drag Jean the last few feet. A police officer stood at the entrance of the building. It was Officer Tim Callahan. Detective Walker knew Callahan. "What's up?" he asked.

Callahan replied in clipped phrases. "Mugger. Medium height, black curly hair, blue jeans, sneakers. Suspect said to wear an I LOVE NEW YORK T-shirt."

"Thanks, Callahan. I'll keep my eyes open."

The reptile house had alligators, turtles, lizards, and many other kinds of reptiles, but mostly snakes. There were big snakes and small snakes, poisonous ones and harmless ones, snakes from the backyard and snakes from distant jungles.

The group was particularly impressed by the two huge brown and tan pythons. They were at least twenty feet long and weighed as much as a grown man. As the zoo keeper passed by, Jean asked him what he fed the pythons.

"I throw them a chicken or maybe a rabbit once in a while," he replied. "Depends on what I can find."

Jean shivered at the thought.

"Don't let them scare you, lady. They may look mean but they're really sweethearts. I pet them all the time. They're very friendly."

"Ugh!" Jean shuddered. "Aren't they disgustingly slimy to the touch?"

"Sure they are. I just wash my hands after I touch them. It doesn't hurt me."

He walked on.

Jean gazed at the zoo keeper with a mixture of horror and admiration. She would sooner shake hands with Captain Hook than pet a python.

Maximilian and Jessica were less impressed with the zoo keeper. Maximilian began to reach for his memo book, but Jessica prevented him. "Oh no you don't!" she said. "You always have all the fun. How about me for a change?"

Jessica had begun to carry a memo book like Maximilian. She pulled out her memo book, wrote in it, and passed it to Detective Walker.

Detective Walker read quickly and disappeared in the direction of the front entrance. There he conferred with Officer Callahan. Together, they approached the zoo keeper. They asked if he would please accompany them to the back office. The zoo keeper refused. "I can't leave the floor of the reptile house. I'm on duty. My boss wouldn't like it."

"Don't worry about your boss," Detective Walker said. "I'll square it with him."

They went to the back office. Like the mugger, the zoo keeper was of medium height and had black curly hair.

"I see you're wearing sneakers. Is that usual for zoo keepers?" Detective Walker asked.

"I can wear anything I want, so long as it's comfortable."

They then asked him to open his jacket.

The zoo keeper did so. Underneath was a T-shirt with an I Love New York slogan on it. He was asked to empty his pockets. They were stuffed with credit cards, cash, and jewelry belonging to the people he had mugged.

Upon questioning, the mugger explained that he had become aware the police were combing the zoo for him. He thought his best chance to avoid being caught was to cover up what he was wearing. A zoo keeper's uniform would be perfect. He tried the back door of the reptile house. It was open. He hid in the closet. When the zoo keeper came into the back room for his lunch, the mugger sprang out of his hiding place and attacked him. He bound and gagged the real zoo keeper and locked him in his closet. The mugger then put on the zoo keeper's uniform jacket over his T-shirt. He went out into the public areas and acted as if he were the real zoo keeper. He even answered people's questions. He had no trouble until he met Maximilian and Jessica.

As they led the mugger away, Officer Callahan thanked Jessica for her help. "Without you, we might never have caught the mugger," he said.

Jessica grinned from ear to ear. She loved compliments.

"Still afraid of snakes?" Detective Walker asked his daughter after they had left the reptile house. "A little," Jean said bravely but not very convincingly.

"That reminds me of a riddle," Detective Walker said. "Why was the baby snake unhappy?"

"I don't know," Jean said. "Why?"

"Because someone stole its rattle."

How did Jessica know the zoo keeper was a fake?
(See page 129.)

11
. . . .

THE CASE OF
The Fantastic Movie Script

What did Benny the Onion want most out of life? More than anything else in the world, Benny yearned to be respected. He had the same dream over and over again. In this dream he saw himself walking down Fifth Avenue and, as he passed by, people turned their heads and said, "Look, there goes that wonderful man, Benny!"

How could Benny get people to respect him? He pondered the question long and hard. He finally decided he would be respected only if he became rich or famous or, better yet, both. Unfortunately, every scheme Benny had ever attempted to become rich or famous had turned out to be a disaster. He had been an art dealer, peddled trinkets of all kinds, invested in tourist attractions, sold rare coins. Nothing worked.

Benny the Onion did have one genuine talent though. He could tell the most heartbreaking stories. People felt so sorry for him they gave him money. But Benny was not content to earn his livelihood in this manner. Who would respect a person who depended on others to feel sorry for him? Benny resolved to keep on trying. Who knows, maybe one day one of his schemes would hit the jackpot, and all his troubles would be over.

Detective Walker and Maximilian were waiting for a light to change on Fifth Avenue, when they bumped into Benny rushing down the street as if he had a million things to do and no time in which to do them.

"Where are you off to in such a big rush, Benny?" Detective Walker asked.

"I'm busy, busy!" Benny exclaimed as he wiped imaginary perspiration from his brow.

Detective Walker noticed Benny clutching a book with a soft dark cover to his chest. "What's that you're carrying?"

Benny stroked the book lovingly. "This is an original manuscript. It was written by my good friend, Coleman Coleman. He is a great writer, perhaps the greatest writer alive today."

"Never heard of him," Detective Walker said. "Did you ever hear of him, Maximilian?" Maximilian had never heard of him either.

"I didn't say he was the most famous writer in the world, only the best." Benny pouted.

"What's the manuscript about?" Detective Walker asked.

"It's a movie script. It's all about life in the Plymouth Colony. You know, the *Mayflower,* Miles Standish, the Puritans, the witchcraft trials, and so on. It is an incredibly fine manuscript. The best I ever read. I own it lock, stock and barrel. Or, at least I will own it—soon as I can pay Coleman Coleman what I owe him."

"Will you never learn, Benny?" Detective Walker shook his head in dismay.

Benny looked offended. "Why am I always treated like my brain was canceled? I tell you Coleman Coleman is a great writer. His manuscript will make a fantastic movie. I just know it." Then Benny turned thoughtful. "Of course, I shall also need the right producer and the right director. I shall also need the right stars. I have definite ideas about which actors would be perfect for the parts. I do hope my producer and my director will agree with my choices."

Detective Walker should have known better than to argue with Benny. There are some people who insist on making their own mistakes even if you can prove beyond a shadow of a doubt that they are making mistakes. All Detective Walker could do for Benny was to see to it that he got hurt as little as possible. "How much did you pay for the manuscript, Benny?" he asked.

"A mere trifle. Coleman Coleman wanted $5,000 for the script. I gave him $100. It was all I had. I promised to pay him the rest just as soon as I sold the script."

"Benny, you must have forgotten to take your smart pills this morning." Detective Walker shook his head.

Benny the Onion was no longer listening. He had a

faraway, dreamy look. "I'm on my way now to see an important producer. He's one of the biggest in the business. I think I'll ask $100,000 for the script. I won't bargain with him. I'll tell him straight off—it's $100,000, take it or leave it. That's peanuts for a script of this quality. I know he'll fall all over himself to get hold of it. The picture will be as classic as *Gone With the Wind*, as sensational as *Star Wars*."

Detective Walker decided to save his breath. Trying to reason with Benny when he was in this mood was like trying to turn off a light bulb by blowing on it.

"Not only does the movie have it all—romance, adventure, action, suspense, color—but it is historically accurate. So many movies take liberties with the truth. Not this one. Coleman Coleman assured me that he carefully researched everything down to the tiniest detail." Benny smiled. "Would you like to hear the story?"

"Why not?" Detective Walker shrugged. "It should be interesting to hear what a $100,000 movie script sounds like."

Benny cleared his throat and turned to the first page. "Our story opens with the great English explorer John Cabot sailing bravely forth in May 1497 from England to explore the unknown. He was the first definitely known explorer from Europe to set foot on the North American coast."

Detective Walker observed Maximilian fidgeting nervously, as if something was troubling him, but he was either too polite or too shy to speak up. Detective

Walker assured Maximilian that if he had anything to say, Benny wouldn't mind if he said it. "Would you, Benny?"

"Why, of course not," Benny replied. "I am always interested in anything Maximilian has to say. He is such a bright young fellow."

Maximilian blushed. "Well . . . uh . . ."

"Speak up, Maximilian. I won't bite," Benny said.

Maximilian spoke quickly, eager to get what was bothering him off his chest. "John Cabot was not English. He was an Italian. His real name was Giovanni Caboto. He merely worked for the English."

"A piddling trifle." Benny snapped his fingers. "I shall make a note of it in the manuscript."

"Next we see the Pilgrims in England suffering from religious persecution. They decide to leave England for the New World where they will be free to practice their religion."

Maximilian was fidgeting again. Benny smiled kindly and asked, "What is it now, young fellow?"

"The Pilgrims fled England because of religious persecution, but they first went to Leiden, Holland. They remained there for twelve years. In Holland they were free to practice their religion as they saw fit. But a group of Pilgrims decided to leave Holland for the New World, because there they would be better able to preserve their English heritage. These Pilgrims did, in fact, sail from Southampton, England, but only because the ship they hired for the ocean voyage set sail from an English port. Your script makes it sound as if the Pilgrims did not first live in Holland."

"More petty details," Benny waved his hand, but no longer smiling. "At least you will admit that the passengers on the *Mayflower* were all Pilgrims."

"Sorry, Benny, but the majority of the passengers on the *Mayflower* were not Pilgrims. They were what the Pilgrims called Strangers. They were called Strangers because they did not share the religious beliefs of the Pilgrims."

Benny sulked. "The Pilgrims first landed on Plymouth Rock in 1620. Even I know that."

Maximilian shook his head sadly. "The *Mayflower* first landed in Provincetown on the tip of Cape Cod, not in Plymouth Harbor. The *Mayflower* reached Plymouth Harbor a full month later. There is even evidence they did not set foot on Plymouth Rock when they got to Plymouth Harbor. The earliest Pilgrim records make no mention of Plymouth Rock. Many historians now believe the story of Plymouth Rock is a legend rather than a fact."

"Okay, *okay!* I believe you. Can I go on now?" Benny said frostily.

"I didn't mean to upset you, Benny. But facts are facts."

Benny continued grimly. "Our story jumps a year. We see the Pilgrims celebrating Thanksgiving. They have invited their Indian neighbors to share their food and friendship in the log cabins the Pilgrims built."

"The Pilgrims did not live in log cabins," said Maximilian. "When they first arrived in the New World, they built temporary shelters, not log cabins. None of the Pilgrims built log cabins in their first settlements because this kind of construction was unknown to them."

Benny's morale was being devastated. He swallowed hard and made a brave effort to continue. "We then see the great witchcraft trials in Salem, Massachusetts. We show innocent people being accused of witchcraft. The hysteria spreads until the entire community is affected. Finally, twenty innocent women are burned at the stake for being witches."

"You are right about twenty people being put to death in the Salem witchcraft trials, but they were not all women. Seven of the twenty were men."

"Big deal!" Benny said ungraciously. "Anything else you would like to insinuate?"

"None of them were burned at the stake. Nineteen persons were hanged. The twentieth victim, Giles Corey, was pressed to death with heavy stones."

What remained of Benny's confidence collapsed. "That doesn't leave me with much of a story, does it?" He sighed. "I guess I've been taken for a ride again." His face wore a beaten-little-boy look.

"I'm afraid so, Benny," Detective Walker said. "There is always the chance, though, I might be able to persuade Mr. Coleman Coleman to return your money. It's worth a try."

"Oh, would you!" Benny's face lit up.

Coleman Coleman lived on the other side of town. They knocked at his door. A small, thin man with a cherry-red nose answered.

"That's him!" Benny burst out. "That's the guy who sold me that fake movie script!" he jumped up and down.

"Take it easy," Detective Walker said to Benny. "You're liable to blow a fuse."

Coleman Coleman looked at Benny as if he were a termite. "Who is this creature?" he sneered. "He should be locked up for trying to impersonate a human being."

Benny sputtered in rage.

"I haven't seen anything like him since the circus left town," Coleman Coleman added with a disdainful snort. "And who are you?" He glared at Detective Walker.

Coleman Coleman was such a sourpuss that if he bit on a lemon, the lemon would make faces.

Detective Walker identified himself as a police officer. "What do you have to say in reply to Benny's charges, Mr. Coleman?"

"Well, for your information, I am a poet. I do not write scripts. I have never written a script. Nor have I ever set eyes on this poor excuse for a human being before. And if I am lucky, I never again shall."

"You're sure?"

"I repeat. I never sold this person a script. Look here, Detective Walker, you are either remarkably stupid or remarkably hard of hearing, or perhaps you are both."

Detective Walker found himself beginning to dislike Coleman Coleman as much as Benny did. "But you did sell Benny a movie script?"

"You really work hard at being difficult, don't you? I just told you, I did not sell him a script."

"How long did it take you to write the movie script?"

Coleman Coleman's blood pressure was inching up. His nose was becoming redder. It was beginning to glow like a light bulb. "For the last time, I did not sell this person a script! I don't know what's eating you, but I hope it isn't catching."

Coleman Coleman was not aware that Detective Walker was using an old police technique for getting information. A suspect is asked a simple question. He is asked the same question over and over again, with minor variations. The pressure is kept up nice and steady. The suspect gets more and more rattled. Finally, he gets so flustered he blurts out the truth.

"How much did you take for the movie script?"

"Look, Detective Walker, I'll try again to get through to you. I will use simple language. I won't make anything too complicated. I never—no never—sold this person a script of any kind. I especially did not sell him a script about Pilgrims. I also did not ask for $100 for the script. Have I made myself clear? Need I repeat it? Would you like me to write it out for you? And please, Detective Walker, the next time you pass my house— pass my house!"

"Mr. Coleman, I do not believe a word you are saying."

"Detective Walker, I have nothing more to add. All I can say is that your mind must be permanently closed for repairs."

Maximilian, who had been listening quietly all this time, began to concentrate. He didn't do so for long, however. He reached for his memo book and began to write in it.

Coleman Coleman watched Maximilian write. "What is he writing?" he asked nervously.

Maximilian handed Detective Walker his memo book. Detective Walker glanced at it and smiled approvingly. "Good work, Maximilian!"

Maximilian blushed.

"Mr. Coleman, I am prepared to give you one last chance. If you return the money you took from Benny, we might forget the whole thing. I believe I am being reasonable."

"Can I first see what the young man wrote in his book?"

"Gladly," Detective Walker said.

Coleman Coleman read Maximilian's memo book. He said nothing but reached into his wallet and returned Benny's money. Benny gave him back the script.

As they were at Coleman Coleman's door, Detective Walker could not resist saying, "This reminds me of a riddle. If the Pilgrims came on the *Mayflower,* what did the barbers come on?"

"I don't know"—Coleman Coleman made a face—"and I don't much care." But then curiosity got the best of him. "What did the barbers come on?"

"On clipper ships!"

Coleman Coleman groaned. "Jokes like that will make humor illegal."

How did Maximilian know Coleman Coleman was lying?

(See page 130.)

12

· · · · · · · ·

THE CASE OF

The Big-City Rustlers

Jessica Wolfe ran all the way to the precinct house looking for Maximilian. She found Peter, her brother, shining a police officer's shoes outside the building. "Is Maximilian inside?" she asked, struggling for breath.

"Scram, Jessica! Who wants you around?" Peter growled.

"Who's talking to you, birdbrain? I was speaking to the officer whose shoes you're shining."

The police officer said Maximilian was at George's Coffee Shop getting coffee and sandwiches for the officers. Jessica thanked him and ran off in the direction of the coffee shop.

She met Maximilian as he was heading back to the precinct house with a carton of food and drink.

"Maximilian"—she gasped for breath and clutched

her side in pain—"there's an unbelievable line around the Check-It-Out Supermarket!" Maximilian suggested that she wait until she caught her breath. When she recovered somewhat, Jessica told him about a line outside the supermarket. It was growing by the minute. "Things could get out of hand," she warned. "There could be a riot. People could get hurt. Better tell Detective Walker right away!"

"Take it easy, Jessica. Why are people so anxious to get into the supermarket?"

"They're selling meat for fifty cents a pound, that's why. Today that's like giving it away. Something fishy is going on. I bet the meat is stolen. Don't forget now, if it turns out that I'm right, remember who told you."

"Sure. If it turns out you're right."

"I better get back and keep my eye on things." And off Jessica dashed again to the Check-It-Out Supermarket.

Maximilian distributed the coffee and sandwiches he brought from George's Coffee Shop. He then told Detective Walker about Jessica's report on the Check-It-Out Supermarket. Detective Walker said there was nothing illegal about selling meat at a low price.

The telephone rang just then, as if on cue. It was the owner of another supermarket down the street from the Check-It-Out Supermarket. He complained that the Check-It-Out Supermarket was selling meat at fifty cents a pound.

"That's not against the law," Detective Walker reminded the caller, repeating what he had just told Maximilian.

"I agree. But no one can sell meat at that price and stay in business. I know what meat costs and what it should sell for. I tell you there is something wrong!"

"How about the quality of the meat?"

"The meat is first-rate. I sell meat like this for anywhere from $2.49 to $2.99 a pound, and then I don't make much. If you want my opinion, I think the meat has been stolen. That's why I am calling the police."

Detective Walker recalled that Jessica was under the same impression. He promised the caller he would visit the Check-It-Out Supermarket.

Detective Walker was overwhelmed by the crush of people he saw at the supermarket. The line stretched clear around the block. Occasional fights were now breaking out as people tried to sneak into line. One enterprising chap even sold tickets. For a fee, he would stand in line for you and buy your meat.

Detective Walker forced his way into the store, not without nasty remarks from people who thought he was trying to cut in ahead of them. Even when he got inside the store, he had to fight his way through aisles jammed with wall-to-wall people. He finally managed to reach the manager's office.

The manager's door was shut tight. Detective Walker knocked. "Who's there?" a nervous voice from inside squeaked. Detective Walker said it was the police. The door opened a crack. The manager demanded to see identification. Detective Walker showed his badge. The manager opened the door. He apologized for keeping the door locked. He said he could no longer take the crowds. The manager wiped his perspiring face and said he was especially happy to see the police now.

"Why is that?" Detective Walker asked.

"Because I've just about run out of meat!" the supermarket manager groaned. "A lot of people have been waiting for hours. I hate to think of how they will react when they find out they've been standing in line for nothing."

Detective Walker recognized the danger. He asked if he could use the phone on the manager's desk. He made a call to headquarters and requested police reinforcements.

Detective Walker began to question the supermarket manager. He wanted especially to know how the store could sell meat at such a low price. The manager explained he could offer the meat at fifty cents a pound for two reasons. First, he bought the meat cheaply. He paid seventy-five cents a pound. Normally, the same grade of meat would have cost him double that, if not more. Second, he offered the meat as a loss leader.

"What's a loss leader?" Detective Walker asked.

"A loss leader is an item sold at a loss."

"But why would you sell something at a loss?"

"To attract new customers and to keep the old ones happy. Everybody loves a bargain. Our motto, in fact, is Check It Out at the Check-It-Out Supermarket. Who knew the response would be so overwhelming? I guess it's the times. Everyone is desperate to save money."

"And did you buy your meat from your regular source?"

The manager of the supermarket admitted he bought

the meat from two men he had never seen before. The men said they were cattlemen from Texas. They told him they raised the cattle, butchered it, and trucked it in—all by themselves. They said they cut out all middlemen and could therefore sell their meat at low prices.

"Can you describe the men?"

"They were dressed in cowboy outfits. They wore those big cowboy hats, jeans, plaid shirts, boots, and belts with large silver buckles. One of them winced every time he took a step. He complained his cowboy boots were too tight."

"How did they deliver the meat?"

"In one of those haul-it-yourself trucks."

"Did you get the license number?"

"Sorry, no."

Police reinforcements now arrived. The crowd was gradually dispersed. Some people did not believe all the meat had been sold. They grumbled about having waited so long in line without being able to buy any meat. Fortunately, there were no serious incidents.

Detective Walker returned to the precinct house. He began to contact the haul-it-yourself truck agencies in the city. No agent reported having rented a truck to two men dressed in cowboy outfits. Detective Walker set the case aside to await further developments.

Being small has its advantages, as Jessica was soon to discover. She was able to pop in and out of the Check-It-Out Supermarket without attracting attention. She was able to come up with an important clue.

She managed to sneak into the meat department in back of the store. There she spotted a few pieces of fat trimmed from the meat on sale. She examined the pieces and found one with its United States Department of Agriculture or USDA stamp number. Every meat packer or warehouse has a USDA number. It is shown by a bluish or purplish stamp on meat. It is possible to trace where a piece of meat comes from through its USDA number.

Jessica passed this information on to Detective Walker. He, in turn, contacted the United States Department of Agriculture. From the USDA number on the scrap of meat, he learned the meat came from a meat-packing plant on Washington Street, on the west side of Manhattan. Detective Walker visited the plant. The meat packer said his plant had been broken into and nearly a ton of meat was missing. One employee of the plant said he had seen a suspicious truck outside the plant. He was able to furnish a description of the truck.

Armed with this information, Detective Walker had no trouble tracking down the truck rental agency and picking up the two men. They were brought to the precinct house. The two men were a miserable sight to see. They both had running noses, headaches, and sneezed mightily. "Ah-choo!" one exploded. "Ah-choo!" the other echoed. It seemed the men had severe colds.

When Detective Walker remarked how unusual it was to see people with colds in such lovely spring weather, the men became flustered. They did not have colds, they insisted. They said they had hay fever. They said their hay fever was caused by ragweed pollen.

"Ah-choo!" one sneezed. "Ah-choo!" the other answered.

Maximilian, who had been listening silently nearby, pulled out his memo book. He had no need to concentrate. He quickly wrote in his memo book and passed it to Detective Walker.

Detective Walker smiled and nodded in approval. "I never saw you solve a case so quickly. Thanks!"

"Don't thank me," Maximilian corrected Detective Walker. "Give credit where credit is due. Jessica is the one who did the really important work."

"You're right," Detective Walker said. "You've done a wonderful job with Jessica. She is fast becoming a fine detective. Please give her my thanks for helping to break the case."

Maximilian said he would be happy to do so.

As the men were being led away to jail, one of them complained his feet were killing him. The cowboy boots he wore were too tight. Could they rest for a moment?

Detective Walker agreed. While they were seated waiting for the man with the tight shoes to recover, Detective Walker said, "That reminds me of a riddle. What do you call thieves who steal chopped meat?"

"I don't know," the man with aching feet said. "What?"

"Hamburglars!"

The man sprang up. "Aching feet are a pleasure compared to having to listen to such corny riddles! I demand to be taken to jail immediately!"

How did Maximilian know the men lied?
(See page 131.)

13

. . . .

THE CASE OF
The Baby Blue Car

Jean Walker's car was in the garage being fixed more often than it was running. Jean had to get another car before the repair bills drove her to the poorhouse. When she went to visit the new car showrooms, the prices made her sick. Even a used car from a dealer was out of the question on her salary. Her only hope was to buy a used car from a private person.

Benny the Onion learned that Jean was in the market for a car. He insisted on helping her. "Your father never hesitates to help me when I need help," he said. "The least I can do is help his daughter."

Several days later Benny phoned Jean. He told her he had found the perfect car. Could she meet him at a small garage on 53 Street that evening? She said she would be there.

At the garage, Jean saw Benny the Onion and a gentleman standing next to a late model baby blue car. Benny greeted Jean and introduced her to his companion. It was the owner of the car, Mr. Reginald Fitzgerald. Mr. Fitzgerald's British accent was so thick you could cut it with a knife.

Jean fell in love with the car. It was exactly what she was looking for. She could hear the car saying, "Buy me!" Jean hoped Mr. Fitzgerald had not caught the look of longing on her face. "What condition is the car in?" she asked sternly.

"Tip-top, first-class, Miss Walker. Please accept my assurance on that account."

"How long have you had the car?"

"About two weeks."

"What!" she said, astonished.

"Allow me to explain. I did not actually buy the car. I won it in a raffle. Oddest thing. I was passing by a chap on the street who asked if I would buy a raffle for the benefit of some charity. I bought a ticket. Next thing I knew, I was informed that I had won the raffle, and I was presented with this lovely automobile."

"I see," Jean said, not sure whether to accept his story. "Why do you want to sell the car?"

"Amazing country, your United States. Here I am, visiting from England on a three-week holiday, never been to your wonderful land before, and I win this automobile. Unfortunately, I have no further need for the automobile after having used it to tour your marvelous country. I already own an automobile back home, you see. To have it shipped back to England would cost a small fortune. I prefer to sell it."

The explanation made sense to her.

"Allow me to show you the finer points of the automobile, Miss Walker. Where is that flashlight?" He fumbled in the glove compartment. He found it at last.

They began at the rear of the car. "See how roomy the trunk is," he said. He was right. The trunk was roomy for a small car.

Mr. Fitzgerald then led Jean to the front of the car. She noticed a dent. "Ah, I see you spotted the dent on the right fender. I got it while trying to park the automobile in a tight spot," he said.

He fidgeted with the catch on the hood. "Always have difficulty opening the hood." He finally managed to get it open and shone his flashlight on the motor. "As you can see, the engine is in fine condition. Notice the wires leading to the spark plugs, how clean they are. That tells you the engine has hardly been used. The automobile gets better than thirty miles to the gallon. A tankful of gas goes a long way."

Finally Mr. Fitzgerald invited Jean to inspect the interior. Jean loved the velvet upholstery. She was disappointed to find no car radio. Mr. Fitzgerald guessed her thoughts. "The automobile did not come with a radio, I am sorry to say." Jean also spotted a small crack in the windshield. "Yes," he said as he saw Jean inspect the crack, "the windshield is damaged. You will have to replace it eventually. But a new windshield shouldn't be too expensive."

Mr. Fitzgerald allowed Jean to drive the car several times around the block. It handled beautifully.

Jean knew this was the car for her, even with its faults. But could she afford it?

Mr. Fitzgerald looked at Jean inquiringly. "Well, Miss Walker, what do you think?"

"Oh, it's all right," she said, trying to sound nonchalant.

"Does that mean you are not interested?"

"I didn't say that. It all depends on what you are asking for the car. I can't afford a great deal." Jean gulped. "How much?"

The figure he quoted was so low, Jean could hardly believe her ears. She asked him to repeat the price. Yes, she had heard right the first time. There had to be a catch, she told herself.

"There is a catch, however," Mr. Fitzgerald said.

Aha, here it comes! Jean thought.

"Since my flight to England departs in two days, I shall have to ask for the entire amount in cash by tomorrow."

"But Mr. Fitzgerald, you really don't expect me to buy an automobile without having my mechanic check it over first!"

"I quite agree. In fact, I shall insist you bring your mechanic along, or anyone else you might wish, for that matter. I have no intention of selling this vehicle to you unless you are fully satisfied it is in perfect mechanical order. If your mechanic approves, and I am confident he will, we can conclude the deal tomorrow evening."

"You won't sell the car in the meantime?" Jean couldn't prevent herself from saying.

"You have my word for it. I shan't."

"Then it's a deal!" Jean grabbed Mr. Fitzgerald's hand and pumped it up and down until the poor man was afraid his arm might fall off.

Jean thanked Benny the Onion for helping her find the perfect car. Benny said it was nothing.

Jean's mechanic inspected the car the following day. He found it to be in excellent condition. She next went to the bank and withdrew money. She then arranged to have her father, Benny, and Maximilian present when she bought the car. They were all to meet at the garage later that evening.

Jean introduced her father and Maximilian to Mr. Fitzgerald. She asked Mr. Fitzgerald if he would mind showing them the automobile. Mr. Fitzgerald said he would be happy to oblige.

"Let me fetch my flashlight," he said, "and we'll have a look, shall we?"

He had trouble with the catch on the hood, as before. "Never can quite get this hood open," he said. He finally managed to open it. Mr. Fitzgerald shone his flashlight on the engine. "Look at the wires leading to the spark plugs. Clean aren't they? The engine is economical on gasoline. Gets over thirty miles to the gallon."

"Are there any problems with the car?" Detective Walker asked. "I'd hate to have them show up later when you are already in England."

"The automobile does have some flaws, but they are

minor. I will be happy to show them to you. The right fender has a dent, as you can see. Also, the windshield has a small crack. As I told your daughter, you will have to replace it eventually. Further, the automobile does not come equipped with a radio. I can honestly say I know of no other problems." He then finished by taking them to the rear of the car. "Note how roomy the trunk is," he said.

Detective Walker was satisfied.

Everyone was all smiles because the matter was so easily settled. The only person not smiling was Maximilian. He found it impossible to accept Mr. Fitzgerald's story. When Maximilian asked himself why he was suspicious, he drew a blank. He began to concentrate hard to find the answer. He concentrated so hard, his brow creased and his eyes squinted. His face soon relaxed. He pulled out his memo book and wrote in it. He then offered his memo book to Detective Walker.

"Well, I'll be!" Detective Walker gasped. "Mr. Fitzgerald, I'll have to ask you to come along with me to the precinct house. You are under arrest."

"I'm what!" he sputtered angrily. "You simply cannot go around arresting people merely because some young scamp scribbles in a notebook. I shall inform the British Embassy at once! I am sure they will lodge a protest with your government."

"Come off it, Mr. Fitzgerald! You know you have a lot of explaining to do. Your story has more holes than a fishnet."

"What's the trouble, Dad?" Jean asked.

Detective Walker showed her Maximilian's memo book. Jean was devastated.

Benny the Onion also read the memo book. His reaction was to look for a flat rock under which he could crawl.

On the way to the precinct house with Mr. Fitzgerald in handcuffs, Detective Walker said, "This reminds me of a riddle. Which part of a car needs the most rest?"

"I don't know," Mr. Fitzgerald said. "Which?"

"The wheels, because they are always tired."

How did Maximilian know Mr. Fitzgerald was lying?
(See page 132.)

14

· · · · · · · ·

THE CASE OF

The Marie Antoinette Necklace

The Jewelry Emporium on Fifth Avenue was one of the most exclusive stores in the world. The store sold only the finest and the most expensive jewelry. Many of the items for sale were not only beautiful, they were often of great historical value. The prize item for sale in the store at the moment was a necklace once owned by Marie Antoinette, Queen of France. It was popularly known as the Marie Antoinette Necklace.

Mr. Pierre Martin, owner of the Jewelry Emporium, truly loved the jewelry he sold. Fine jewelry gave him joy such as did little else in the world. Were it not for the fact that he had to pay rent and salaries, Pierre Martin would have preferred not to sell many of his favorite pieces of jewelry. He would rather have kept them for his own pleasure. When a particularly fine piece of jewelry was sold, he was often depressed for days.

Not only was the jewelry in the store carefully selected, so were the customers. One did not pop in from the street and expect to buy things in the Jewelry Emporium. Mr. Pierre Martin would permit someone to become a regular customer only after that person demonstrated a proper appreciation for fine jewelry. Money had nothing to do with it. Many an upstart with money, but without taste, was shown the door and asked never to return again.

To be a steady customer of the Jewelry Emporium meant that you had arrived socially. The honor of being a regular customer of the store was passed down from generation to generation like a choice box at the opera. And the more selective Pierre Martin became about customers, naturally, the more people clamored to become customers. The Jewelry Emporium, as a result, never lacked for customers.

The distinguished and fabulously wealthy Baron von Hoffenstein visited the store. He was looking for an appropriate birthday gift for his wife. Pierre Martin personally waited on the baron.

The baron asked to be shown the Marie Antoinette Necklace. Pierre Martin fetched the necklace from the store vault. He carefully removed the necklace from the tissue paper in which it was wrapped and set it down gently on a black velvet cloth. The baron gasped at the lovely sight. It was the most exquisite object he had ever seen in his life. He stared so long and so hard, Pierre Martin was afraid the baron might wear his eyeballs out.

When discussing the possible purchase of an item such as the Marie Antoinette Necklace, one did not rush things. Pierre Martin allowed the baron all the time he needed to take in the lovely details of the necklace. Only after Pierre Martin sensed the baron was ready to tear his eyes away, would he dream of speaking.

Pierre Martin twisted the ends of his moustache until they became fine points. "The necklace, my dear baron, consists of twelve rubies of three carats each. Rubies of this size are extremely rare. I am sure you are aware, my dear sir, that carat for carat, rubies are more valuable than diamonds."

The baron shook his head.

"The rubies are surrounded by sixty-two diamonds of at least a carat each. The historical importance of the necklace I need not discuss. I am certain your taste is sufficiently elevated to appreciate its unique importance."

"Thank you!" the baron said, touched by Pierre Martin's flattering words.

"Only because you are an old and valued customer would I consider passing the ownership of the Marie Antoinette Necklace to you. It is, as you yourself must see, a supreme example of the jeweler's art."

"I am overwhelmed by the great honor you have shown me by deeming me worthy to be considered as a possible owner of the Marie Antoinette Necklace."

Only after these graceful formalities were concluded was price mentioned. Pierre Martin asked $1,500,000 for the necklace. One did not bargain in the Jewelry Emporium. It was considered bad form. You could either afford the price—or you could not. To the baron, the sum of $1,500,000 was a mere trifle. However, he did request a moment or two to consider the matter. Pierre Martin was understanding. He stood aside and twirled the ends of his moustache while the baron thought it over.

The necklace had been given to Queen Marie Antoinette by her husband, King Louis XVI of France. It was a birthday gift. That the baron might give his wife the very same necklace would make her extremely happy. Of course, the baron smiled to himself, people might also compare him to Louis XVI. The baron made up his mind. He wished to be the new owner of the Marie Antoinette Necklace. Wordlessly, he took out his checkbook, filled out a check for $1,500,000, and handed it to Pierre Martin.

Pierre Martin accepted the check and sighed. He knew he would be depressed for days, once the necklace left his store. Pierre Martin put on a brave face. "Would you care to take the necklace with you, or shall I have it sent?" he asked.

"Please send the necklace to my home," the baron purred contentedly.

Pierre Martin said he would see to it. He escorted the baron to the door and bowed deeply to the departing baron.

The necklace was placed in a fine box and entrusted to Lewis for delivery.

Lewis had worked for the Jewelry Emporium for nearly forty years. He had been the principal designer of the store, and in his time, had been one of the finest. However, several years ago his hands began to stiffen from arthritis. He was no longer able to design jewelry. He was now reduced to doing errands around the store. Still, he was content. So long as he was surrounded by fine jewelry, he felt life was worth living. His passion for fine jewelry was at least as great as that of Pierre Martin, if not greater.

Many times over the years, Lewis had resented the sale of particularly fine jewelry to those customers he deemed to be undeserving. For example, he did not approve of Baron von Hoffenstein. Lewis did not think the baron was sufficiently sensitive to fine jewelry.

After thieves had made several attempts to break the store windows, it had become standard practice for the Jewelry Emporium to display imitations. Each window had a little sign saying, Imitation Jewelry Only. Thieves would not bother to break windows to get at mere imitations.

Lewis was supposed to deliver the necklace the following day. Without asking anyone, he switched the necklaces. Baron Hugo von Hoffenstein would get the imitation necklace. The genuine Marie Antoinette Necklace would go right back into the store's vault. Lewis expected the baron would not be able to tell the difference.

Lewis was right. For over six months, there was total silence from the baron. Then Pierre Martin got a phone call. It was the baron. "You swindler, you!" the baron hissed through clenched teeth. "You are nothing but a common thief!"

"I, a common thief!" Pierre Martin recoiled in horror. He had been accused of many things in his life, most of them stemming from his preference for jewelry over people. But never, no never, had the slightest breath of scandal ever attached itself to his good name. Pierre Martin suppressed his indignation only with a supreme effort. He said he would be right over.

The furious baron, eyes blazing with anger, opened the door to Pierre Martin. He flung the necklace in Pierre Martin's face. "Here is the worthless piece of junk you sold me! Ah, if only these were the good old days, I would challenge you to a sword duel and make mincemeat out of you!"

Pierre Martin examined the necklace. The baron was right. The necklace was an imitation. Pierre Martin was puzzled. How could the baron have owned the necklace for over six months and not know it was an imitation? "When did you discover the necklace was an imitation?" Pierre Martin asked.

"My wife wore the necklace to a dinner party last evening. One of the guests at the dinner party, a friend of long standing, is an expert on jewels. When I said my wife's necklace was the Marie Antoinette Necklace, he laughed in my face. He informed me the necklace was an imitation, and not a particularly good one at that."

Pierre Martin drew himself up to his full height of five feet, sucked in his stomach as well as a man could who was as wide as he was tall, and declared, "In that case, sir, I must inform you that I truly regret having sold you the Marie Antoinette Necklace! Anyone who cannot tell the difference between a genuine necklace and a fake one does not deserve to be the owner of the Marie Antoinette Necklace."

Pierre Martin wrote out a check for $1,500,000, and handed it to the baron and took back the imitation necklace.

Detective Walker was assigned to the case. He visited the baron and learned that Lewis had delivered the necklace, or rather, the imitation. Detective Walker next went to the Jewelry Emporium to talk with Lewis. Maximilian came along.

Lewis gave the police little trouble. He freely admitted he delivered a fake necklace to the baron. When asked why, Lewis explained that he had been mugged by two men on his way to the baron. The two muggers made off with the real necklace. He said he went back to the Jewelry Emporium and substituted the fake necklace for the real one taken by the muggers. He made the switch because he was afraid he might lose his job. He thought the baron would not notice the difference, and that the baron would be just as happy with the fake one as with the real one.

When Pierre Martin learned the Marie Antoinette Necklace was now in the hands of muggers, he shrieked in horror and promptly fainted. Lewis helped to revive

Mr. Martin. He tried to calm his boss. This made Pierre Martin even more upset. "The Marie Antoinette Necklace is missing, and you dare tell me to keep calm!" Pierre Martin fainted again. A doctor was fetched. The doctor ordered Pierre Martin to bed. He would not be allowed to get up for at least a week. His nerves had been shattered.

Detective Walker continued questioning Lewis. "Did you get a good look at the two muggers?"

"Not really. They came up from behind. They stuck a gun in my back and ripped the necklace out of my hands. They told me not to turn around if I didn't want to get hurt."

"And did you do as they said?"

"You bet I did! I didn't want to get shot. I read in the papers all the time of muggers who kill people for a few dollars. I hate to think of what they would do to get their hands on something like the Marie Antoinette Necklace."

"Did the muggers talk among themselves? Did they have any accent or voice mannerism? Even the tiniest detail would be helpful."

"The two muggers did not talk among themselves, as I recall. Now that I think of it, I only heard one of the muggers speak. He had a deep voice. His voice sounded authoritative, like someone who is used to giving orders. That's all I can really tell you. You understand, Detective Walker, it all happened so fast and I was so frightened, I was not as observant of details as I should have been."

"That's all right, Lewis, I understand."

While Detective Walker was busy taking down Lewis's account of the mugging, Maximilian was also writing in his memo book. Maximilian handed his memo book to Detective Walker when he finished writing. Detective Walker read the memo book with admiration for the speed with which Maximilian cracked the case.

"Lewis," Detective Walker said, "I have reason to believe you were not mugged."

Lewis did not seem to be surprised by the charge. It was as if he expected to be caught. He seemed to be relieved it was all over, in fact. "Just to satisfy my curiosity, Detective Walker, how did you find out?"

Detective Walker showed Maximilian's memo book to Lewis. He was impressed. "Maximilian is right, of course. That young man is a superb detective."

As usual, Maximilian blushed.

"This reminds me of a riddle," Detective Walker said. "Where can you find the biggest diamond in the world?"

"I don't know," Lewis said. "Where?"

"On a baseball field."

How did Maximilian know Lewis was not mugged?
(See page 134.)

. . . .

SOLUTIONS

. . . .

· · · · · · · ·

THE CASE OF
THE DANGEROUS SIDEWALK

All that could be seen of the bag lady's injury was a black-and-blue mark on her right shin. There was no blood. Yet, Dr. Melvin R. Harris said the woman had a compound fracture. Her leg was broken in two places, he insisted.

Maximilian knew that the difference between a simple and a compound fracture is a question of whether the broken bone has pierced the skin and not the number of breaks.

A simple fracture is a broken bone that has not pierced the skin and is not exposed to the air. A simple fracture may be a bone broken in more than one place. A compound fracture, Maximilian also knew, is a break in which the bone has pierced the flesh and is exposed to the air. There is often blood around the wound where the bone has cut through the flesh. A compound fracture may be a bone broken in only one place.

Any genuine doctor would have known these facts. Maximilian concluded that Dr. Melvin R. Harris was a fake. The fall had been staged to squeeze money out of Mr. John, owner of the Cinderella Beauty Salon.

118

• • • • • • •

THE CASE OF
THE THIRTEENTH
RICHEST MAN

Lucas said H. Henry Hunt had told him what had happened before he died. H. Henry Hunt said he surprised a pair of burglars as they were ransacking his library. He could not tell who the burglars were because they wore masks. He was certain it was a man and a woman, however.

Maximilian spotted the flaw in the story. If H. Henry Hunt had surprised the burglars who killed him and then fled, the body would have landed on top of the scattered papers and books. Instead, as was the case, some of the books and papers were on top of the body. Maximilian concluded there was no burglary. The murderer first killed Mr. Hunt and then scattered books and papers all over the room, some of which landed on the dead man's body. The murderer was trying to cover up his crime.

Lucas had hoped that by planting the story of the two masked burglars, the police would suspect Babs the Bag Lady and the fake doctor. Lucas had not counted on Maximilian's magnificent brain.

119

• • • • • • •

THE CASE OF
THE GRAFFITI PHANTOM

Sluggo accused Maximilian of being the Graffiti Phantom. Maximilian had, in fact, a black Magic Marker in his possession. However, this in itself was not conclusive evidence. Sluggo said he knew Maximilian was guilty because Sluggo arrived in the hallway a few minutes before Maximilian. Rather than proving Maximilian guilty, this only led Mr. Patterson to suspect that Sluggo had enough time to put the graffiti on the wall himself.

Maximilian recalled what he had read in a book on graphology, the study of handwriting. He remembered that, contrary to what most people think, hand printing is actually more individual and specific than is handwriting. People who have reason for covering up their trail often think that by using hand printing it would be harder to trace them than if they used handwriting. The opposite is really the case. It is much easier to identify hand printing than it is to identify handwriting.

Maximilian printed MAXIMILIAN STINKS! on a sheet of paper. Sluggo was asked to do the same. Mr. Patterson then compared the graffiti on the wall with the two samples of hand printing on the sheet of paper. He could immediately see who the Graffiti Phantom was. It was Sluggo.

Sluggo would have kicked himself—if he could. Maximilian had outwitted him again.

• • • • • • •

THE CASE OF
THE CROSS-EYED GAUCHO

Benny the Onion said that in March 1888, his great-grandfather saved the life of the American ambassador to Argentina in a raging blizzard. As if to lend weight to his story, he added that a record-breaking blizzard also hit New York City on the same date, March 12, 1888. Maximilian verified the date of the blizzard.

Maximilian found Benny the Onion's story ridiculous because the seasons in North and South America are not the same. They are reversed, in fact. When it is winter in the United States, it is summer in Argentina, and vice versa. March may be our winter season, but it is the summer season in Argentina. Maximilian concluded there was no snowstorm. The story was purely make-believe.

Why the seasons are reversed can be easily understood. The earth's axis is tilted at an angle of slightly more than 23 degrees. When the tilt is towards the sun, the rays of the sun strike the earth's surface more directly, and it is summer; when the tilt is away from the sun, the rays of the sun strike the earth's surface less directly, and it is winter. While the Northern Hemisphere tilts towards the sun, the Southern Hemisphere is tilted away from the sun, and vice versa. Thus the seasons are opposite.

Maximilian's brain was stuffed with facts of this kind. They helped him solve many a case.

• • • • • • •

THE CASE OF THE MISSING TEN COMMANDMENTS

Mr. al-Malik said he was a religious man, a true Mohammedan. However, Maximilian was aware that Muslims do not use the term "Mohammedan" in referring to their religion. Modern Muslims find the use of the term "Mohammedan" or "Mohammedanism" objectionable because it leads Christians and others to suppose that Muslims worship Mohammed. Muslims worship God alone, or Allah, as they call God.

Moreover, Maximilian knew that Muslims are not permitted to eat the meat of a pig, let alone enjoy it. A true Muslim would gag on bacon, which, of course, comes from pigs. Mr. Ibn al-Malik was no true Muslim. His story was a lie from beginning to end.

To add insult to injury, by the time the check had arrived, Mr. al-Malik had already left the coffee shop. Jean ended up having to pay for his bacon and tomato sandwich.

· · · · · · ·

THE CASE OF
THE AMATEUR COIN DEALER

Benny the Onion said he gave the man a $15 deposit for three Roman coins. Benny said the coins were denarii. There was such a Roman monetary unit. Benny pointed to a date on the coins as proof that they were ancient. The date on the coins led Maximilian to the opposite conclusion.

Maximilian knew that dates were not used on coins until late in the 1400s. If a date appears on a coin, the coin cannot be ancient.

Also, the coin read CLXXX B.C., meaning 180 B.C. However, before the Christian era, there could be no such date as B.C. Only after the Christian era came into being, could there be B.C.

Finally, all the coins were alike. Maximilian knew that no two ancient coins were precisely alike because they were made individually by workmen using only an anvil, a punch, and a mallet. The size and shape varied greatly because the lump of metal would spread out differently each time. Only modern machinery could produce identical coins. Hence, the coins were modern.

Benny the Onion never did find the man who sold him the coins. He was out $15.

• • • • • • • •

THE CASE OF DOUBLE TROUBLE

Lem Huggins claimed he was at the dentist's having a tooth filled at the time of the robbery. His dentist confirmed that Lem Huggins came to his office at 3:30 P.M. and left at 4:30 P.M. The filling itself was done around 4:00 P.M.

The elevator operator, on the other hand, was certain this was the same man who hit him over the head and robbed the warehouse. He gave the time of the attack as 3:30 P.M.

How could one person be in two places at the same time? Of course one person could not be in two places at the same time. Suppose, however, two persons were involved. Suppose, further, the two persons were so alike they could easily be mistaken for each other. This would explain everything. Maximilian concluded it was a question of identical twins.

As Maximilian reconstructed the crime, it was Clem Huggins, not Lem Huggins, who struck the elevator operator and broke into the warehouse. This was at 3:30 P.M. By 4:00 P.M., Clem Huggins was out on the street peddling the stolen 64K chips. All during this time, his brother, Lem, was having his tooth filled at the dentist.

What broke the case? Clem Huggins made the mistake of inviting Peter and Benny to join him in a snack. He had a steaming bowl of lamb stew. This was around 4:00 P.M. By 4:15 P.M. they had finished eating. However, a person who has a filling is not supposed to have hot food until at least an hour afterward. The earliest he could have had hot food would have been 5:00 P.M. Therefore, Maximilian concluded, the person whose tooth was filled and the person who committed the robbery were not the same—even if they looked exactly alike.

Ever since they were children, people mistook one for the other. When the brothers grew up and chose a life of crime, they used this fact to get out of jams. One brother committed the crime; the other brother furnished an alibi if the first brother was picked up by the police. It had always worked. That is, it had always worked up until now.

．　．　．　．　．　．　．　．

THE CASE OF
PROFESSOR MARVELLO
THE GREAT

Miss Lee denied she had tried to steal the cashbox, at first. She then said it was Professor Marvello the Great who put her into a trance and commanded her to steal the cashbox. She said she was powerless to resist. Was it fair to punish her for something for which she was not responsible?

Professor Marvello the Great made his living by entertaining people with flashy stage effects. He could make a woman think she was eating a tomato when she was eating an onion; he could make a man think his mouth was on fire when he puffed on a cigarette. But these were basically show business tricks. Within minutes after leaving the stage, the woman would be quite able to tell the difference between a tomato and an onion. The man who smoked would only too soon go back to smoking without feeling his mouth was on fire.

Maximilian was aware that many people held false ideas about hypnosis, including Miss Lee. Some of these false ideas come from the movies. In many horror films, the bad guy is portrayed as having great hypnotic powers. He merely stares into the eyes of his helpless victims, generally pretty girls, and they fall under his total control. They are then supposed to do anything he demands, whether they wish to or not. This is pure nonsense.

Maximilian knew that it is impossible to hypnotize a person and force him to do anything that goes against his standards of conduct or his sense of right and wrong. You cannot make a person who believes killing is wrong commit murder. Similarly, you cannot make an honest person steal.

Miss Lee, who had only been with Professor Marvello the Great for a short time, was not aware of these facts. She did not understand the nature of hypnosis or its limits. She said the first thing that came to her mind, hoping this would get her out of trouble. Instead, it backfired.

· · · · · · ·

THE CASE OF
THE MISSING GAG FILE

Three things bothered Maximilian about Howie Dixon's story.

First: The window in the library was supposed to have

been smashed by thieves who broke in from the outside. It is a fact that when a window is broken, the glass pieces tend to fly in the direction of the blow. Thus, if the thieves had smashed the window from the outside, the glass pieces would have fallen inside the room and onto the rug. Instead, the broken pieces were found outside the window. The window, Maximilian concluded, had been broken from the inside.

Second: It was raining hard on the night of the robbery. Howie Dixon said the gag file was stolen some time during the night while he was asleep. The rain would have come through the broken pane and damaged the rug. However, the rug was not damaged. Maximilian guessed the cardboard had been placed over the broken pane as soon as it was smashed. Thieves might not have worried about the rug. The owner of the rug certainly would have.

Third: It would have taken at least two men to walk off with the file. The men were supposed to have entered from the street. Maximilian asked himself why the rug was not tracked up by the thieves. The rug wasn't tracked up because no one entered from the outside.

After being shown the evidence, Howard Dixon admitted he staged the robbery. He meant no harm, he insisted. The gag file was safely stored in a closet in back of his apartment.

Why did he do it? The running feud between Howie Dixon and Fred Lewis, even in the good old days, was never real. They discovered that their feuding gave them lots of free publicity. They had their names in the newspapers and magazines all the time.

There now was a renewed interest in old-time comedians, especially among young people. Why not revive their old feud? It had worked before. Why wouldn't
it work again? They decided to stage the gag file robbery.
Howie Dixon would accuse Fred Lewis of the robbery.
The media would then pick up the story. Their names
would be in the headlines again.

When Howie Dixon learned that Detective Walker
liked riddles of all kinds, they began to exchange riddles.
They would have stayed up half the night comparing
riddles had not Maximilian complained about having
school the next morning.

· · · · · · · ·

THE CASE OF
THE FRIENDLY PYTHONS

Many people think that snakes are slimy. It is not hard
to understand why. For one thing, the skin of a snake
is shiny. It has a wet look, like a person with oily skin.
For another thing, many people view snakes with horror
and disgust. Since repulsive creatures are often slimy,
many people conclude that snakes are slimy as well. We
even think of some people in such terms. For example,
a truly evil person is called a slimy snake.

The zoo keeper said he often petted the pythons. When Jean suggested that they were slimy to the touch, he did not disagree with her. He said he merely washed his hands after touching the snakes.

Jessica once owned a snake. She knew better. She knew that snakes are perfectly dry to the touch. Anyone who handled snakes, such as a zoo keeper of a reptile house, would know that. Jessica concluded the man who said he was a zoo keeper was an imposter. He was the mugger the police were looking for.

. . . .

THE CASE OF
THE FANTASTIC
MOVIE SCRIPT

Detective Walker asked Coleman Coleman over and over again if he had sold Benny a script. He repeatedly denied it. As the questioning continued, Coleman Coleman grew increasingly irritated. He thought he was not getting through to Detective Walker. Exasperated to the breaking point, Coleman Coleman was not aware he was giving himself away. He blurted out revealing details. He said he had never sold Benny a script about Pilgrims. Neither Detective Walker nor Benny had said what the script was about. How did Coleman Coleman know the script was about Pilgrims?

Also, Detective Walker asked Coleman Coleman if he had taken any money from Benny. He repeatedly denied that he had done so. He finally said, losing patience, he had not taken $100 for the script. How could Coleman Coleman have known the exact amount when no one mentioned the figure?

Coleman Coleman knew the script was about Pilgrims and that he had taken $100 from Benny because he was guilty.

. . . .

THE CASE OF
THE BIG-CITY RUSTLERS

The two men said they did not have colds. They insisted they had hay fever. They said their hay fever was caused by ragweed pollen, the most common cause of hay fever in the eastern part of the United States. Maximilian knew that the ragweed season in the eastern part of the United States occurs in the fall. This was spring. The two men were not suffering from hay fever, Maximilian concluded. They had common colds.

Why were they so anxious to deny they had colds? If they admitted they had colds, they might be linked to the robbery at the meat-packing plant.

The two men had no trouble breaking into the meat packing plant. They parked outside the plant for two days in a row. They observed the comings and goings of plant employees. When they were sure that all the plant employees had gone home, they smashed the lock on the door and entered.

They had planned everything carefully except for one small detail. They had forgotten to dress properly for the freezing temperatures in the refrigerator lockers in which the meat was kept. By the time they had finished carrying off the meat, they had developed sniffles. They thought it would be smarter to say they had hay fever rather than colds. They had no idea hay fever was seasonal.

• • • • • • •

THE CASE OF
THE BABY BLUE CAR

Mr. Fitzgerald said he had never been to the United States before. He was visiting on a three-week holiday.

Yet, as Maximilian observed, Mr. Fitzgerald used American automobile terms, not British ones.

For instance, Mr. Fitzgerald used the word flashlight. In England, a flashlight is called a torch or an electric torch. Mr. Fitzgerald referred to the trunk of the automobile. In England, the trunk of an automobile is called a boot. He also spoke of the hood of the automobile, which he had trouble in getting open. The hood is known as a bonnet in England. Also, in England, spark plugs are known as sparking plugs.

Again, Mr. Fitzgerald admitted the car had no radio. In England, a radio is called a wireless. Also, Mr. Fitzgerald pointed to a dent in the right fender. A fender is known as a wing in England. Finally, he said the automobile was easy on gas. In England, gasoline is called petrol.

Maximilian reasoned that a visitor to the United States might use an American word or two. However, all the automobile terms Mr. Fitzgerald used were American, not British.

It turned out that Mr. Fitzgerald was the head of a ring of car thieves. The car, of course, had been stolen.

. . . .

THE CASE OF
THE MARIE ANTOINETTE
NECKLACE

Lewis said he had been attacked by two muggers. They came up from behind, stuck a gun in his back, and warned him not to turn around. When Detective Walker pumped Lewis for further details, Lewis said that only one man actually spoke. He had a deep authoritative voice. If Lewis had not turned around, how could he have known there were two muggers?

Also, Maximilian observed, Lewis did not seem to be upset by the incident. When Pierre Martin learned the Marie Antoinette Necklace had been stolen, he shrieked and fainted away. His doctor ordered him to bed. Maximilian learned that Lewis was even more fanatic about fine jewelry than his boss. Lewis was calm, Maximilian concluded, because Lewis knew there had been no mugging and that the Marie Antoinette Necklace was safe.

When confronted with these facts, Lewis made no attempt to hide his actions. He said he was proud of what he had done. If a similar situation arose in the future, he was prepared to do the same thing, even if it meant going to jail. He would do anything to prevent important pieces of jewelry from falling into the hands of upstarts and other undesirables.

Pierre Martin was overcome with joy upon hearing the real necklace was safely locked in the store vault. He popped out of bed and was soon his own self again. Not only was Lewis not fired, but Pierre Martin gave him a handsome raise.

These days Lewis and Pierre Martin can often be found crooning over the rare beauty of the Marie Antoinette Necklace. They vow they will never part with the necklace until a perfect buyer comes along. This could take years—they hope.

As for Baron Hugo von Hoffenstein, scratching his name off the list of regular customers of the Jewelry Emporium gave Lewis and Pierre Martin the greatest pleasure.

ABOUT THE AUTHOR

Educated at the University of Chicago and at Rutgers, Joseph Rosenbloom served for many years as director of public libraries in New Jersey, before leaving in 1974 to become a full-time writer. He lives in Brooklyn Heights, New York.